To Millie

Life, DEATH And Other Characters

Another Anthology Of Short-Short, Micro And Flash Fiction

By

Geoff Le Pard

With all my love

Geoff Le Pard

About This Book

Over the last few years, I have written a lot of flash and short fiction, often in response to a prompt. These pieces cover pretty much every major genre apart from YA, MA or children's fiction. This selection was written during 2019. Dip in and enjoy them; better still, let them inspire you to write your own.

Copyright, etc.

For more information about the author and upcoming books, please visit geofflepard.com

Send In The Clouds

Celia Pomeroy pressed the intercom. 'Yes?'

'Mrs Pomeroy?'

Whoever was at the front gate sounded cheerful. Celia wished she could muster such bonhomie.

'It's Rebecca. From Landscape Cleaners. Skies, views and aspects are our speciality.'

'Lands...? Oh, are you here about our aspect?' Thank heavens, she thought. Hosting Gerald's business contacts would be hell enough without the right view to set everything off.

'That's right. We'll soon have you shipshape and visually credible.'

'Do you want to drive round the back and I'll show you what we need.' The girl – Rebecca, was it? – had better be as good as she'd heard. Pulling on her sou'wester and heavy-duty wellingtons, Celia headed for the back of the house.

As she emerged from the French windows, Rebecca was easing herself out of her van, clutching an enormous umbrella. She smiled enthusiastically. 'How can we help? You said you'd spoken to some party planners?'

Celia wrapped her arms around herself, trying to shrink inside her coat. 'We bought this place a few weeks ago, but we had no idea that might happen.' She waved at the trees. 'I mean, who'd do that?'

Rebecca squinted where Celia had pointed. 'I'll go and check in a moment, but from here, I'd say sprites or possibly sprites and tree faeries. Didn't the vendor mention the need to pay them fealty?'

'No.'

'It's pretty standard. You should take it up with your lawyers. It's something you'd expect to be disclosed when they do their inquiries.' She peered at the troubled branches again. 'That weaving is pretty recent, so we should be able to unknot everything and then defrustigate your arbours.'

'Will this fealty cost much? We've lived in the city up to now, so I've no experience of these rural practices.'

'Oh no. A few bowls of milk and a daily newspaper. That should see them right. What else?'

'The sky? The party planners told me it needs a clean.'

Rebecca looked up. 'It is pretty scuffed and rumpled. We'll reel it in, give it a good wash and shake and then rehang it. Don't worry; when the boys put it back, they'll tuck it in and no one will know it's been down. We can iron it, but some people think it looks a bit too perfect. Are the planners aiming at rustic or sophisticated?'

'Sophisticated with a supercilious overtone.'

'Then we'll iron it. If it's too flat, give us a call and we'll have someone puff it out a bit.'

Celia began to relax. 'I'm so glad you came.'

'It's why we're here.' Rebecca licked her finger and stuck it into the air. 'This wind is fairly boisterous. If you're aiming at sophisticated, shall we tone it down?'

'Is that easy?'

'It should be. We can add in some bespoke zephyrs to accompany the coffees and liqueurs, if you like. Maybe you should raise it with the planners and let me know.' She grinned. 'I'll just take a few pictures and measure up. Why don't you go back inside? It's a bit chilly out here.'

'Yes, I'll do that. Oh, one other thing. I wondered if you knew anything about flowers.'

'Flowers?'

'A friend told me it's the latest addition to the best organised parties. You have arrangements and bouquets and all sorts.'

'Really? No, I've not heard this. How does it work?'

'Well, it did sound a bit fantastical.' Celia giggled. 'The way I heard it, there are these specialists - flowerists, I think they're called - who buy in a lot of cut flowers and -'

'Cut? As in severed from their stalks?' Rebecca took a step back. 'That sounds barbaric!'

'It does a bit, doesn't it? I think we'll stick to the tried and tested. One final thing. Do you do moon dimmers? I've heard we're in for a full moon on Saturday and I don't want it detracting from the light show.'

'It's not a service we offer, but I have a good contact at Lune In A Tic, who provide all your lunar requisites. I'll give you their number before I leave.'

'Marvellous. I'm making coffee. Would you like a cup?'

'Lovely.'

Little Helpers

'I hate this time of year, you know.'

'I'm not listening, Elvis.'

'I don't ask to get picked, Ernie, but I always am.'

'It's a privilege. Errol's never had a turn.'

'He can take my place any time.'

'Don't be silly. The missus chooses. You know that.'

'Yeah, but why is it always the same people? You know it's true. Eric, Elrond, Edward…'

'It's because we're good at what we do. And those lads love it. Look, they're nearly running.'

'Yeah well. I'd be happier if they left me in jigsaws. I've found my niche in jigsaws.'

'Don't you get bored, cutting up the same pictures year after year?'

'Nope. The patterns are always different. Do you know there are two hundred and seventy-one million permutations?'

'You're as boring as everyone says.'

'Thanks. Maybe if I was chummier, I wouldn't get this de-icing gig.'

'You know it's not that. It's them.'

'My hands?'

'Of course your hands. There's no one else with hands like yours. The missus says you were sent by a divine gift when you appeared with those hands.'

'Ernie, can I ask you a question? It's a bit personal.'

'Go on.'

'I've been thinking. It's just because of something Ethelbert said, after last year's Freeze. Something about why the fellas don't treat me like they do the others.'

'You don't want to believe what he says. You know he's been in toy trains too long, don't you? Keeps losing track.'

'Yes, well, it's just it made a bit of sense, see. Do you think the boys hold it against me, what I do with my hands?'

'Do?'

'Where they go?'

'They know someone has to, erm, do what you do.'

'Yes, sure, but until I came along it wasn't the same each year. It was shared around, yes?'

'True. Everyone got a turn.'

'And it's not like people were crying out for that turn, was it?'

'Well, no, it wasn't exactly a privilege, but given your gifts, we could all see it was your destiny.'

'I really don't want to do it this year. Maybe I could do his ears and - '

'Noooo. No, that's not the attitude. You're so good. If any of the rest of us tried it would take weeks. You can knock them out in a couple of days.'

'But still, it's not exactly how one wants to be remembered, is it? It's one thing to be part of a special elite chosen by Mrs Claus to go and dethaw Santa, ready for the Christmas delivery; it's a bit different to be known as the hot-handed elf who each year melts Santa's balls.'

'You can hardly leave them frozen, can you? It'd be like having a pair of maracas clickety-clacking every time the sleigh hits a bit of turbulence. If that didn't wake up all the kiddies, I don't know what would.'

'I suppose…'

'Come on, cheer up. The sooner you get his gonads glowing, the sooner you can get back to those puzzles.'

It Doesn't Matter What You Do, So Long As You Dress The Part

Margery Strool opened the door with her hip, her hands full. The Prime Minister's office seemed empty. 'Gerald?' Where the hell was he? 'You wanted a word about tactics for the meeting with the POTUS and... Oh shit, no.'

Gerald Marlene emerged, arms wide open. 'What do you think?

Margery deposited the files. 'So, this is how we restore the Special Relationship, is it?'

'See,' Gerald adjusted the holster. 'This is how I see it. Chuck is from Milwaukee, right? He's all good ol' boys and rhinestones, so this,' he waved a hand at the embroidered waistcoat, the chaps and the dusty boots, 'will make him...'

Think you're a pillock, Margery thought but didn't say.

Gerald spun the Stetson towards an ormolu hatstand. It missed. 'Georgie Bush did it with Tone.' He affected a cod-American accent, 'Yo, Blair.'

Margery slumped on the sofa. 'He'll think more yo-yo than yo. We should focus on policy -'

'Boring.'

'Or the new head of NATO -'

'Dullsville.'

Margery peered with a jaundiced eye. 'Do you need one of your pills?'

Gerald tutted, practicing a quick draw that sent the six-shooter across the room and into a novelty coal scuttle made from a troll's foot, gifted by Norway. 'I like this approach. Homely.'

'Why not ask him what he wants to talk about?'

'Oh sure. That's the verbal equivalent of tickling a man with diarrhoea. Come on, you're my PPS. Who's after Chuck?'

'The German chancellor. And no, you can't wear your lederhosen. You know that's reserved for party conferences and undecided voters.'

'My Brunhilda? I could use the false breasts the last chap left?'

Margery turned away, wondering what she'd do when he realised he was down for dinner with a party of shamans from Easter Island.

When Living The Life Isn't All It's Cracked Up To Be

Extract from the Hades Herald series: *"Time Fillers For Infinity: Jobs For The Dead". Interview conducted by Temerity Plain.*

Zelda Bywater is a Portal Management Volunteer who has been helping the recently departed to cross over since her own demise during the exceptionally foggy spring of 1911, when she erroneously mistook the herd's bull for its prized milker and gripped what turned out to be very much not a teat.

Zelda, you're a translucent. Does that help you as a PMV?

Oh, indeed. Being so transparent helps those who've just experienced the shock of transmission to see what's ahead.

Literally?

Exactly. They don't realise how exposed they are on crossing. I'm there to make sure there are no untimely incidents with the pre-dead. Some have called it their first out of body experience and, if they don't cross quickly, there's the possibility of an interface and no one wants that.

How do you make sure they know what to do?

Oh, well, that's where the training comes in. When you volunteer to be a Portal Manager, you're given your mighty orb-staff…

The lollipop?

Staff, please. We've moved on from such over-glucosed appellations. Those who are passing are used to the imagery of the woman with the disc-pole indicating a crossing from their predeceased existence and so tend not to notice how, erm, d… d…

Dead?

Diaphanous they are. It's a bit of a shock, all that absence of substance thing. Seeing me, positively sheer against this gorgeous back display...

It's lovely, isn't it?

Willian Morris was a volunteer one time, so they say. The Powers That Were don't like unnecessary adornment, given that aesthete vibe they cultivate, but they thought this worth keeping. It mesmerises most newcomers and they are drawn into the Pre-Portal Zone.

Can you explain to our subscribers what the Pre-Portal is? They may not remember.

No, quite. There's a lot to absorb on your first day in the Afters. The Pre-Portal is like a waiting room at the doctor's, only with more flowers and less oxygen. It's here you're directed to the specific After that will be home to your next phase. My role is to see you safely installed and ready for your interview. I like to think I can help take their minds off what's happened as well as what's ahead.

Do you have many problems?

Well, naturally there are the disbelievers, the how-do-I-go-back-crew, but most are pretty sure what's going on. Some even ask about my time; it's natural to try and find some comfort from someone's actual experience.

You don't tell them, do you?

Gosh, no, Temerity. If I learnt one thing in my training it's that it's taken years to get the Living to stop all this science knows best malarkey and embrace fake news. Just as well since the established religions have been losing their grip on feeding the credulous a diet of hope and bombast. If they found out that for most of us it's just a lot of sitting about, staring into your void, they'd work harder at staying put and then who'd do this job?

Quite. Thank you, Zelda, for explaining your role. Next week, we will be joining Dennis Conundrum who has just volunteered to join the ranks of the Grim Reapers. As Dennis will tell us, the training before you can become a Reaper, learning the art of breaking the ultimate in bad news, is hard and not everyone gets a sickle. Until then, stay dead!

Finding A Way

Delphine Tombola knew from primary school that the faith she would embrace would need to provide her with a complete and comprehensive way of living. She dabbled with the four major religions and dropped them once they revealed their inherent internal contradictions. Others came and went in clouds of controversy and complications. She explored the thoughts of yoga and shamanism without success. For a while, Jediism seemed the answer , but when her mentor, a plumber, offered to draw her away from the Dark Side through the inappropriate application of his light saber, she moved on.

That's when she stumbled on the tenets of veganism, a faith so simplistic yet so all-encompassing that a natural evangelist like Delphine knew she'd found her calling.

She created a new persona, including a heraldic shield (turnips sinister entwined around a courgette rampant) and a hairdo best described as "distressed kale".

Her pride was her sacred allotment and her determination to ensure the purity of her vegetables. The compost was free of all animal waste, the power to her shed was vegan-certified and nothing leather was allowed on her little piece of heaven.

It came as something of a shock, therefore, when she found out from her neighbour, something of a local historian, that prior to being allotments the site had been an overspill graveyard. Although the neighbour assured her all the bodies had been removed, she couldn't shake the idea that some molecule from a decayed deceased might have found its way into one of her beloved potatoes.

It was all too much. She needed something certain, something simple, something that would give her a clear purpose in life. That is why, finally, she gave herself, body and soul, to the Leave campaign. After all, she mused over her cocoa, what could be simpler than organizing Brexit?

God Service

Margery Plankton pushed her spectacles up her nose and read the letter again. When the postman delivered it, she had been instinctively dribbloidle with anticipation. The last letter she had received – she ignored those which demanded amounts of money she didn't have or offered to make her amounts of money she couldn't imagine - had been from her Uncle Herman and had contained his toenail clippings with a demand she tell him if they were normal. Sometimes being the only podiatrist in the family was a burden, especially as she had to tell him it was only a matter of time before his toenails became carnivorous and ate his leg.

Now, though, she wondered if the tickle of excitement had been warranted.

First, this letter was written by someone who appeared to have only a shaky acquaintance with the concept of cursive handwriting, which elongated her retinas rather painfully. Second, the contents were the last thing she needed right now.

Dear Ms Plankton

God Service

Please note that from the 22nd inst to the next incursion of Jupiter, you will be required to undertake God Service. Please report to the nearest portal on the 21st inst for basic training. We recommend you wear comfortable shoes, elasticated trousers and bring a sweet confection.

This letter is randomly generated in accordance with the Deity (part-time support) Ordnance and complies with all universal laws of chaos, uncertainty and gratuitous bloody-mindedness. Any complaints should be swallowed and used as paperweights. Injury and/or death are/is inevitable, so we recommend you keep your insurances up to date.

Truly yours

Gerald, Servile and Unctuous Groveller to his Stupendence Almitio, the Great God of Bureaucracy

Note: you will find your nearest portal in any one of the following wheelie bins: the blue, outside no.13; the brown, by the King Kong; and any one of the green bins that have congregated alongside the canal. If planning on utilizing the brown, we recommend double thick marigolds.

After Margery read the letter to Millicent, her colleague, she noted how she delicately raised one plucked eyebrow. 'At least it's not more mementos from your uncle,' she opined.

Margery shook her head. 'That might be preferred. Do you think I should try and cry off?'

'Noooo. Just go with it. How bad can it be? How long is it for?'

Margery squinted at the letter. 'Until the next incursion of Jupiter. Whenever that is.'

Millicent flicked through the desk diary. 'I think this time it's the fourteenth after the decennial apocalypse.'

'Sorry?'

'A week on Tuesday. Though it'll seem longer.'

'Oh heck! And this weekend I was planning on making marmalade.'

'You're right though. You can't not go. They aren't very happy if you try and dip out. Look at Old Mrs Gubbins.'

'How is she?'

'I think she finds the cat flap a trial at her age. Someone said they misheard her when she told the god's representative not to get familiar. Does it say which god you'll be?'

'No, just to go to the nearest portal.'

'You know to wear comfortable clothes?'

'It says that in the notes. I'd better go and pack. I start tomorrow.'

'We won't miss you. That's one good thing.'

'For you. I hear time-condensing can be exhausting. Ten years there is a week here.'

'You'll be fine. And if they do duty-free, I'd love a creamy patina of ambrosia with nectar afternotes.'

'I've not tried it.'

'Oh, you should. It makes my skin autumnal and my joints are indescribable.'

'Have you been having problems with your knees again?'

'Not those sorts of joints; it ulanfrumigates my cannabis plants. Oh, and don't forget to take your uncle's clippings. They got out of the envelope this morning.'

'Oh goodness. No harm done I hope.'

'Not too bad. Mrs Spigot was in to have her proximities degreased when they got out. She'll need a few extra sutures, that's all.'

Twenty-four hours later, and dressed in Swedish cotton and molasses, Margery slipped inside a green wheelie.

'Oi, do you mind?' The bin flapped its lid angrily.

'Aren't you a portal?'

'No, I'm not a bleedin' portal. You part-time gods have no -'

The bin next to the one Margery was standing in chortled. At least it sounded like a chortle, but it could just have easily been a badly rusted axle. 'Stop teasing her, Meldroyd. It's okay, love. Course he's a portal. Just kick the bottom -'

'Don't you dare kick my bottom. You just... ow, that bloody hurt.'

Margery hated possessed plastics. They were always getting uppity, something to do with having deregulated carbon atoms. But she knew better than to be anything other than polite as she slipped through the base and into a white tiled corridor that smelt of lavender and Tuesdays.

A headless receptionist turned her torso in Margery's direction and then popped her head onto the counter. 'Sorry, dropped a lens. Domestic or international?'

'Er... I...'

The head's expression morphed into something approximating agony with a tincture of sympathy. 'Or is it God Service?'

Margery nodded.

'Then take the impossibly fiery arch, third on the left. There's anti-burn cream and optional self-skin grafting on the other side.'

'Wouldn't it make more sense to have the cream this side of the flames?'

The head smiled. 'Yes, of course it would, but that's hardly going to pass the utterly random and capricious test, is it? Now off you trot and keep your hands by your sides. There's a special offer on gratuitous amputations this month. Unless you're looking for a new set of digits? We have some fabulous Witchity Gnarled just in and a snip at two organs or a dozen curses a set.'

Margery stuck her hands in her pockets and started off, but the head called her back. 'Did you bring a confection?'

She lifted her arms. The head wiggled its eyebrows. 'Molasses impregnation? Prudent. Laters.' With that the hands lifted the head off the counter and it disappeared.

Margery wasn't inexperienced. She'd had to visit HQ before, ever since she found out about her other self, as Xenata, Goddess of Equality, Diversity and Being Mildly Content With Your Lot, one wet holiday in North Norfolk. It hadn't been so much of a shock as an irritation. How could she possibly be a "goddess" if she was covering equality and diversity? But her pleas to be classed as a godbeing had fallen. She knew, of course, that she was a god of some kind, ever since she had found she could conjure up a light whenever she needed it and that whenever offered a sandwich, the crusts detached themselves with a grovelling apology.

'Xenata? Good to see you.' A smiling Ovoid with pink cheeks and a chestnut fondant topping spoke in an irritatingly upbeat sing-song voice as it floated up to her, now she was through the arch relatively unscathed.

'Zunder? You doing God Service, too?'

Zunder, God of Timekeeping, did something that in Ovoids equated to a smile. 'No, I'm in charge.'

Margery sighed. 'Why do you need me?'

Zunder oblated. 'You understand feet, yes?'

She nodded slowly.

'I seem to have grown this.' From behind his globular form a stumpy leg and foot emerged.

'How?'

Zunder's colours became even more vivid. 'I was minding my own business when Zeus appeared, saw me and told me to hop to it.'

'And you what? Asked him how?'

'Something like that.'

'So he cursed you?'

'Can you do anything? This is so embarrassing for a smoothly cool spheroid like me. I mean, a limb! Yuck! Your speciality is feet, isn't it?'

'If it's a Zeus curse, you'll need someone to take it over.' Margery pursed her lips. 'It's a bit of a long shot, but my uncle has developed Weretoe.' She scribbled a number on the side of Zunder's new leg. 'Call him. He'll help.'

'How so, if I need someone willing to take this curse off me?'

'I think, between him and his toes, I can safely say they'll probably bite your leg off for it.'

Between A Rock And A Sore Place

'Morning, Captain.'

'Morning, Staff. What's on the agenda today?'

'I'm really excited about the first one. It was in the quiz the other night…'

'Bit of a geek, aren't you?'

'No, listen, Captain. This is cool. Name five of the fourteen planetary inter-actions that have almost led to galactic conflagrations. Obviously, there was the massacre of Stromboidal Five and the erroneous demolition of the Subcretinous star system, but do you know the rest?'

'Peabody's alternative?'

'What was that?'

'Commander Peabody reassigned the gender of every male to female in the Parsimonious Group to try and remove their aggressive natures.'

'What happened?'

'Oh, massive civil strife, pandemics, you name it.'

'Why?'

'The queues to the toilets became enormous and evolved into a new group of single cell organisms, which attacked each other. It was dreadful.'

'Interesting. Any more?'

'Not that I can recall. I'm guessing our target isn't one we've mentioned.'

'No, go on. Have a guess.'

'Nope. Come on, let's see the itinerary. What's that? Dearth? Is there something lacking on this piece of rock?'

'Dearth? No, sorry, sir, that's a bit of my breakfast. There.'

'Earth? Never heard of it. What are we meant to do?'

'Oh, I'm sublimating with excitement, sir!'

'I can see the stains, Staff. Do you need a moment?'

'A tissue, maybe?'

'There. Go on.'

'Well, this Earth is a bit of a lump, as you say, but it is one of the few places where the mineral Brazilian appears occasionally, and our sensors have identified that another piece has secreted itself to the surface.'

'Okay. Let's see the terms of engagement.'

'That's the point, sir. We must avoid engagement at any cost.'

'Okay, so do we have a plan?'

'Of course, Captain. In the next hour we will set in motion a weather modifier, which will cause a dreary bleak snow shower to cover the rescue site. Apparently, no one will come out in these conditions, other than the odd weirdy who takes pictures of wet snowflakes…'

'Do their inhabitants do such a thing?'

'It's a ritualized homage to their harsh roots. That and the dog needs a walk.'

'Right. So, the weather sets in, we collect the rock and that's it?'

'Indeed.'

'So, come on, why did the last lot nearly cause a mass conflict?'

'Oh, one of those unfortunate misunderstandings. It was at the time when every collection fleet was under instructions to contact local life forms and create a good first impression.'

'All a bit new agey. Did they chant?'

'I believe they implanted the concept of yoga into the local sub-coreal cortex of a shaman.'

'I didn't think they still did that stuff.'

'It's been banned for a while, but there are still pockets where it's been resistant to eradication. Anyway, the captain in this case - Pretentious Oddicky - did the "We come in peace, yada yada" shtick and explained to their High Representative - erm, let's say a Mrs Grommet, who was there to greet him - that he would be in and out in a nano. He just needed to sort out the Brazilian if she could point him towards where he might find it.'

'Didn't his sensors say?'

'It was part of the initiative back then to ask first. Anyway, the High Representative knew what he meant, but it turned out to be the most awful trap. She led him and the reception group to what they assumed was this interrogation centre - Deirdre's Tan and Wax Boutique - where they removed the crew's grenoidal oomfangles with the most gratuitous piece of torture ever recorded in the known galaxy. Naturally, Oddicky called for backup, war was declared and sides were taken.'

'What happened?'

'Some jobsworth at HQ did some research and found out it meant something totally different on Earth and they did this stuff to their own kind who volunteered for it. So, uncivilized as it might seem, they couldn't be blamed for imposing it on others.'

'Takes all sorts, I suppose.'

'Some people think getting your drong refusticated is a bit much.'

'Hard to credit, eh? And they all grow back eventually.'

'Yes, same with these Brazilian thingies. They get them time and again.'

'Madness. So, avoid the locals bearing wax gifts, is it?'

'Always wise, sir.'

Outsized

'Gee. Look at the colour of that.' Betty had her hands on her hips.

'Opalescent, I think it's called.' Pat stood a few feet back, studying the map.

'Milky green. Like some radioactive mistake.'

Betty turned and glared at Dot. 'Have you no soul? It's beautiful.'

Dot stuck out her tongue and joined Betty on the ridge of moraine. Both women regarded the tarn in silence.

Pat, meanwhile, approached the edge with care. She stood a few feet behind and just below the other two. 'It's just the light reflecting off the rock flour that's suspended...'

Betty spun round. 'You're almost as bad. It's just pea soup for the giants that live here.'

'Giants? What have you been drinking?' Dot leaned forward slightly. 'Mind you, that looks like clothing, doesn't it? It's a shirt, surely. There.'

Pat and Betty looked where she was pointing. Pat was the first to speak. 'It's just ice; part of the Angel Glacier. Probably came down in the hot weather we had last week. Bloody climate changes. If I could get hold of the buggers who won't sort it...' She made to strangle an imaginary politician. 'Though...' She, too, pointed and let out a stifled giggle. 'They're knickers. For sure.'

Betty clapped. 'You are smutty, Pat. If Roger could hear you now...'

'He'd run a mile.' Both Dot and Betty laughed, though Pat didn't join in. She said, 'It's probably lichen. Either that or someone needs to give them a good wash.' She turned back to her guidebook. 'Maybe it's to do with the legends. It says this is the bathing pool of Saskatchewan giants who lived here ten thousand years ago. When the dinosaurs died out, they hid in the mountains.'

Betty nodded again towards the water. 'How come a giant could hide?' She shook her head. 'Mind you, the woman who owns those knickers – now she must have an arse on her.'

Pat turned away, her face colouring. She wished she'd never mentioned the knickers. 'Come on, ladies; we've a few miles to do today.'

Dot hurried after her. 'You never know, we may find a not-so-micro thong hanging in the pine trees.'

*

As the three women turned the corner by the last of the lateral moraine, Hulga pulled herself away from the glacier and bent down to the water to pick up her knickers. As she did so Huf detached himself from the side of Mount Edith Cavell and collected his shirt. 'We need to be a bit more careful,' he said as he pulled it on before unhooking his breeches from the large aspen.

Hulga twisted round and looked down. 'Do you think my arse is big, Huf?'

Huf considered both the question and the arse. After a few minutes he said, 'Yes. You're a giant.'

'But big for a giant?'

Slowly to begin with, but with increasing speed, as a tree might as it toppled over, Huf swung his hand and smacked said arse. Hulga giggled her rumbling giggle as sheets of ice slipped from the mountain side and into the Tarn.

*

Betty turned at the noise and looked back down the path. 'Another piece of the glacier lost, I suppose.'

Pat pulled a face. 'It makes you want to smack someone, doesn't it?'

Busted

Fragrance Pourboire crossed the parquet to where Jonas Umbilical waited, camera swinging from his wrist in what was rather too obviously irritation. 'They're ready, Jonas.'

'About time. I haven't all day just for some publicity shots, you know.'

'Sorry, but it's... well, it's tricky.' Fragrance glanced nervously towards the door to the changing rooms.

Jonas sighed theatrically, his focus on the tripod in front of him. 'Bunch of prima donnas, I suppose. Can't work out what to wear?'

'Not exactly...'

Jonas glanced up. 'Not another set of glamour pics? I think I've had enough of bouncing busts for one day.'

'Well, there are a couple of busts, but they're not bouncing.'

Jonas nodded knowingly, his attention now trained on the lighting. 'Been enhanced, have they? Goodness knows why they bother getting them enlarged. Makes them look completely unnatural if you ask me, like they've been turned to...' he stopped, his mouth dropping open, 'stone.'

Fragrance turned and followed his gaze. Slowly, indeed almost imperceptibly, the next group of models began to emerge from the door at the far end of the hall. If their movements were laboured – "glacial" was the word that popped into Fragrance's head - the accompanying noise was deep and continuous.

Jonas was quickly by her side. 'What the f... flip? Are they... statues?'

'Technically, they're Caryatids and Atlantids.'

'You what?'

'They're supports.'

'Geez. I'd hate to see the main act. Is there a stage strong enough to hold them?'

Fragrance tutted and moved towards the first sculpture, a marble Adonis holding a red rose. 'Shall I take that?'

With micro-movements, but a sound like a cliff collapsing, the enormous figure stretched out its arm and gently dropped the flower into Fragrance's hand. A single tear emerged from the blank eye and bobbled across the scratched cheek.

'You okay?' As soon as she spoke, Fragrance regretted it as the monument began the laborious and essentially destructive process of nodding. Both Jonas and Fragrance watched in growing horror as the head at first shook and then detached from the unfeasibly muscled torso, before dropping with a crash to the wooden floor and then rolling with almost deliberate care into the centre of the floodlit arena where all the cameras pointed.

Jonas sighed and moved to his customary position. 'You were right, weren't you?'

'Sorry?' Fragrance glanced at the photographer, confused.

'You told me the busts weren't of the bouncing kind.' He pointed his camera. 'Okay, darling,' he addressed the head, 'can we ditch the tears and crack a smile?'

The Just Right Royalty

Gruinard the Abashed couldn't complain. Not really. After all, as was constantly pointed out by the Court Sycophants, he was Heir to the Throne, commonly considered a dish, comely of aspect and sturdy of build. He held a pose; he profiled especially well in the setting sun and his beetled brow was universally said to be as fine and as rugged as any in the kingdom.

And yet, Gruinard wanted none of this adulation. He wanted none of the consequent fawning and genuflecting and gratuitous oohing and ahhing that followed him around Castle Comfy, his ancestral home.

His parents despaired. Queen Opal the Alright and King Glean the Sorted wanted nothing so much for their son as to feel at ease. Of course, he would have to do some ruling one day, but beyond some choreographed wrist waving and the occasional proclamation, the role of Sovereign was no more taxing than, say, having a mole removed, necessary though that was to ensure the royal lawns remained pristine. That's what they had Lord Chamberlains for. They were the ones who did the solemn and weighty stuff. No point being a Monarch if all you got was a peasants' revolt and an ulcer.

Therefore, after one especially painful Royal Flaunt, at which Gruinard hid behind the curtain, the King and the Queen sat with their principal advisor, Lord Stern of Countenance, to discuss that regular worry of all fictionalised fairyland monarchies: "What must be done?"

It boiled down to two possibilities: on the one hand, give the boy what he wanted (King Glean) and on the other, make the boy do what has always worked in the past (Queen Opal).

'He must be allowed to find himself.'

'He must be found a wife.'

Lord Stern did some fairly impressive frowning and emitted a couple of pretty telling harrumphs before opining, 'Both are required.'

And so, it came to pass. Gruinard was given a year to go forth and spend time as an unroyal, spreading oats and other grains in an agricultural rite of passage, while the Queen swiped right, left and centre in the hope of stumbling on a suitable match.

Twelve months passed and Gruinard plied the females and scattered his good seed all around (later, this was misheard by a deaf minstrel who penned the royal dirge "He ploughed the fields and scattered the good seed all around"), before ceasing his Royal Roistering and heading for home.

His mother waited for him. She looked appalled. 'Gruinard, get in there and get yourself ready. Look at your hair. Do something. You'll be wed in an hour.'

Gruinard sat in his chamber and considered his lot. All things considered, he was okay. A bit tired but, yes, he was ready to be Kingly and marry. He picked up his Royal Sword and a strand of hair. No, he'd keep the tresses as a memory of his gap year. Instead, he turned the sword round and began to clean his nails. It was the least he could do.

When Getting Your Roots Done Is Just A Protest

Whip Willow and Twigs Birch stood, aghast.

Twigs spoke first. 'Did you know?'

Whip shook convulsively. 'Just there was this old lady who needed her roots doing. Nothing like this.'

'She doesn't need a prune; she needs a digger. How can she manage with them so... so...?'

'Exposed?'

'Extraneous. And whose roots are those? That old fella? He's not even the same species. Oak and Ash. Have you ever done a male's roots?'

'Darling, you know I haven't. Who called us in?'

'Oh, one of those Second Age Sylvanians. Apparently, Ash – she's the old lady – has been moaning at night and the warden was worried about her roots.'

'Well, quite.'

'Thought she might have a fall and at her age...'

'Could be fatal.'

'Exactly. But I think that stupid Beech on reception -'

'That's not nice, Whip. I know there's a bit of negativity about her...'

'Beech, darling, I said Beech.'

'Oh, sorry.'

'That's alright. Rowan, isn't it? I think Rowan misunderstood about the roots; thought she wanted us to frimp her foliage...'

'You do frimp beautifully.'

'Thank you, sweetness. So, the Tonsorial Tree Tweakers are dispatched in error.'

'We ought to do something. Cover her up a little. I mean, it's rather unseemly. At her age, don't you think?'

Whip nodded and shuffled forward. 'Hello? Ash, is it? How are you?'

The old lady groaned, twisting left and right.

'Just a mo, lovely. I need to try and loosen some of these knots. Terrible they are.'

An almighty crack and her canopy quivered briefly.

'There. How can I help?' Whip tried to avert his eyes from the show of stems and stalks that curled by his trunk. 'We, that's Twigs and me, wondered if you needed a hand. A bit of cover, you know.'

Ash's crown tilted forward. 'Upset you, do they? They're natural, you know. Even you have roots.'

Whip shuffled self-consciously, burying himself a little further into the loamy earth.

'Thing is, Whip, me and the Bl'oak here are a mite fed up with all those saplings hustling us for space, saying there's room for another one. We've been here a long time. You can't live in overcrowded conditions and thrive. It ain't natural. So, we decided to pull up our roots and show them just how much space we need. And, if they don't like a flash of the fleshy bits, well they can go and plant themselves somewhere else. It's a protest movement we're starting.'

Whip tugged at Twigs' trunk, easing her away. 'I think we should go.'

'They've got a point, you know.'

'Maybe, but I'm a tree dresser, not an arboreal anarchist. What say you we get ourselves a sappuchino and see what's next?'

The Road To Hell

Roger Penstick didn't begrudge helping his old friend.

It had been hard watching him slip into that cloudy state where the absent-minded forgetfulness that meant you couldn't remember where your car keys were became the tormented senility that meant you could no longer remember what they were for.

At nine every morning he let himself into the small cottage Arthur called home and met his friend in the kitchen. The carers had already been, made sure he was dressed and fed and left him in his comfy chair for Roger and their morning's constitutional.

'Where shall we go today, mate?' he asked, hopeful of getting some sort of reply. Occasionally, he was offered a smile, sometimes a "Lovely sun" or "Where's Madge?", his long-deceased wife. It mattered not. Not these days. It was all about giving him those fragments of pleasure he could still access.

Arthur didn't really cope with walking far, not these days, but he seemed happy enough to settle into the wheelchair provided by the surgery. Roger manoeuvred the "beast" through the narrow door and onto the path, before encouraging Arthur to sit down and be tucked in.

Roger wasn't that young himself and the short, steep incline wasn't as easy as it used to be. By the time he'd reached the ornamental gates, he was red in the face and short of breath. Sometimes he would mutter to himself, cursing the placement of the Peace Gardens that Millennium money had funded. He couldn't deny, however, how well it had settled to be part of village life, how established the roses and lavender borders now appeared.

But, were he being honest, he would have preferred a walk into the village itself, not this way. They could have sat outside the shop, chatted with those going about their morning affairs, maybe slipped into the Coach Inn for a coffee. There were several pluses to taking that route, not least that it was flat.

He chided himself with this uncharitable thought. The effort was worth it for the enjoyment Arthur got. He clearly loved it here. And it kept Roger fitter than the pub would.

They entered the gates and already Roger could feel his friend sit up. Someone told him those whose minds were closing in sometimes found memories in other senses, in song or, in this case, scent. The fragrance of the early roses was replaced by the saturated delights of the lavender.

'Pretty amazing, isn't it?' he offered as he wheeled the chair so it brushed against the overhanging pendulums of blossom. He saw his friend's shoulders heave, aware a tear would be forming on his lids, his nose beginning to run.

What memory was it he now accessed with such a deep passion? Whatever it was, Roger was pleased to bring even a moment's joy while he still could.

And Arthur?

What would he have said if he could? How would he have explained the tears?

'Bloody hay fever.'

The History Of English-Speaking Statues

Robinson Balustrade held up a hand. The crocodile of year four's finest came to a messy stop. 'Alright, everyone take off their packs and... Yes, Prentice? Toilet? Try the ash tree... The one that looks like Mrs Worple after she's taken you for music on Thursdays... No, Dolly, she doesn't look like an alien with constipation... Where did you learn that word? Mrs Petticoat, eh? Well, you shouldn't listen when someone is in the ladies, should you? Yes, Mrs Jacobite may listen in, but she's the Head. It's part of her job... You're done, Prentice? Good, so... No, Prentice, I don't need proof...'

Momentarily, Robinson's attention was distracted by two of the girls, who were apparently intent on some kind of dental examination of Nathaniel. Having prised them away, he was drawn back to Prentice.

'Yes, Prentice. That's very impressive. Yes, it does look like Mr Crimple's left ear, Nathaniel. No, it's not quite as brown, Dolly, is it? Please, everyone, you can study Prentice's stool later. We have an interview to conduct so... Careful, Prentice, Naomi has... No, Naomi, I'm sure that was an accident. The stool? I don't know where it's gone and right now...' He took a breath and lifted his eyes to Irony Pendule who was bringing up the rear. 'Did you see where it went?'

She smiled. 'Happily not.' She clapped her hands to gain their attention. 'Now, everyone, just unpack your headphones and let's see what we can find.'

Robinson didn't wait, knowing yet more interruptions were inevitable. While his colleague helped the stragglers with their equipment, he headed towards the statue. He stood to one side while Irony jollied them towards him. Unexpectedly, while there was some fidgeting, they all soon settled and stared at him with the sort of rapt attention normally reserved for the moment after one of Mr Jollife's unexpectedly sonorous farts during assembly. He raised his eyes to Irony, who was carefully bringing up the rear with her usual mix of dainty footsteps and novelty whistles. 'Did you say something?'

She smiled the sort of smile that was normally seen carved into hagiographic statues of saints. 'I just said they were sure to learn some new words today.' She grinned. 'Something naughty.'

Robinson gave the children a small bow. 'Maybe. Now, who do we have here?' He put a hand on the ancient stone figure. No one spoke.

Robinson nodded. 'Indeed, no one knows precisely. He's probably a monk from Middle Marsh Monastery.'

'Did a witch turn him to stone?'

'That's a good question, Primula. I don't know, but you could ask him?'

'Can I?'

'Well, we'll try. We… Prentice, what are you doing? You found it? Well done, but please go and put it under that bush. Mrs Pendule has some wipes.' A look passed between them. As the children faced him and couldn't see her, she stuck out her tongue. Teach you, he thought as she followed Prentice and his stool to the disposal area.

Robinson shifted his gaze back to the rest of the class. 'Some clever scientists have found a way of accessing the vibrations of certain types of stone. What we are going to do is see if we can hear them. It's possible they may be words. If it is the monk, he might tell us, Primula.' He took out his own earphones. 'Please, everyone put them on your head like this. And then,' he raised his voice, 'take the end of the wire and place it against the stone. No need to crowd, there's plenty of space.'

Robinson waited. These new agey ideas were all very well, but he doubted they'd hear anything. He stared at his own Amplisender. It looked very neat, but surely it was just gimmicky…

Felicity Panhandle was first to be ready, as usual. She pressed the small sucker against the stone's surface. Robinson watched her indulgently as she listened and frowned.

'Is it? Why don't you move, then?' The small blonde girl scratched the back of her hand. 'Are you sad?' She nodded.

Just then Irony and Prentice returned. 'How's it going?' she asked.

'Look at Fizzy. She's rapt.'

'Are you hearing something, Fizzy?' Irony bent to try and unknot Tarquin and Nathaniel.

Felicity concentrated on something and moved the sucker around the statue's feet. 'Here?' She nodded as she scratched at some moss with her fingernail. She turned to Irony. 'He wants us to move his feet.'

'Sorry?'

'His feet hurt. They're damp.'

'His what?' Robinson began before stopping himself. 'Who are you talking about, Fizzy?'

'The abbot.' The girl tapped the stone. 'He says he's an abbot and he's a...' she frowned, 'I think he said he's a marmite to his feet. He wants to know if we can move him.'

Robinson thought there must be a trick involved, but the small girl couldn't be part of it, not willingly. He glanced around, but they were on their own. He checked on Irony, who was looking at him, wide-eyed. She had put on her earphones and held the sucker to the surface. This was not helping his rising sense of panic and it didn't get any better when she jabbed a finger at his set, pointing at the statue.

As he placed the sucker to the surface, he felt his heart do the sort of summersault only attempted by the Chinese in high diving or his brother on his eight-year old's trampoline after eight pints and a vindaloo.

'...for seventeen centuries and I have to say... Hello, is that Mr Balustrade? Welcome! I was just talking to your class and Ms Pendule.'

'Who is this? Is this you, Irony?'

'Ms Pendule is, I would guess, as stunned as you given the erratic nature of her breathing. No, my name is Carshalton O'Brian and I was Abbot of Marsh Monckton in the fourth century.'

'I... but... how... were you... when...?'

'I know. Tricky, isn't it? I don't suppose you've given much thought to alluvial reincarnation, have you? Bit of a sod... sorry, children... ending up embedded in granite. Comes from relying on a noviciate to do the incanting. Still, you get used to the slow. Everything is slow, really, mostly. But the damp, now that is a trial. If someone could dig a drainage ditch, I'd be most grateful. Or put me on something impervious. No chance you brought a spade, I suppose?'

'No, sorry. We could make it a class project.'

'Really? That would be awfully kind. Maybe prop me up a bit, too. I've slipped over the centuries and until that metal steamy thing came, I had a lovely view.'

'Metal... do you mean the train?' Robinson described it.

'Yes, probably. I could tell the children some stories. How'd you like that, eh? How we converted Hector the Unfazed by cauterising his colon with a red-hot poker up the -'

'Splendid. They'd love that. Meanwhile, I think we'd better be getting on.' Robinson stared around wildly, hoping to discover who was playing this clever but unsettling trick on him. There was still no one to be seen and Irony looked as discombobulated as he felt.

'There's one small thing you might do before you go?'

'Yes?'

'Round the back. Only take a moment, but I'd be eternally grateful if you could maybe use a finger to scratch the lichen out of my buttock fissures. Itch to all buggery, don't you know.'

'What the actual f -'

Irony snorted. 'I told you they'd learn some new words.'

Robinson looked at the wide-eyed children and the apparently statuesque abbot, sighed deeply and dug out his pen. It may be made of stone and it may only be lichen, but if someone was playing a trick, there was no way he would be caught on camera, scratching away at even a representation of a butt crack, with his own finger.

Getting The Job Done

John Plont scanned the cafe, before joining Harry Pettimoron. He fitted the IV line and sighed. 'You well?'

Harry frowned. 'Missus was a bit runky and the mutt had a touch of the dribblets. What do we have today?'

'Have a look.' He handed over a worksheet.

'A couple of underwibbling grommoids and another of those leaking photorombollons.'

'More photorombollons? Nasty buggers. Last one nearly jellied my tooblocket. Helen was dead unimpressed.'

'I bet. Hadn't she just had her scroombottles reframbrigated?'

'Yeah. And her nails done.'

Harry nodded. 'Colin's having a management hang-in, see if we can't get double-wonders next time. Let's do the photorombollons first, then we can warm our prantiles on Mrs Patterson's froomdogle.'

'You think she'll have some of those refragranced zip-zoomers? I could murder a couple.'

Harry rubbed his stomach. 'I'll pass. My orifices are clagging. Come on.'

John released the line, burped and floated after Harry to their truck.

'So, holiday plans?'

'Oh, the usual. We've giving the mother-in-law to medical research again - they're taking some cuttings from her hippocampus - and the kids' school has organised a time warp for their history project before they build an alien lifeform at the Other Species Camp.'

'What base material do they use these days? Silicone? Carbon?'

'Zinc-based ginger with a cardamom isotope. You get peace loving bipeds with low flatulence and good posture. We're here.'

Once the scaffo-magnets were in place they set about sealing the light leak.

'How did this happen?' Harry wrestled with the parallel dimension.

'Some office do. Someone snagged the fabric of time with their party heels.'

John steadied the magnets while Harry stitched the hole shut.

'You?'

'Doris said we should take a cruise. Jupiter's good value since they reupholstered its Red Spot. 'There. Time for a break.'

'Nice.'

The Erosion Of Hope

For longer than people knew, the two metal figures had stood sentinel, staring out on to the North Sea, watching, forever watching, those tumultuous waves. They weren't ancient, but their origins were unknown and many a passerby, hoping for some information plaque or storyboard, were disappointed to find no guidance as to their history. Who, or what had placed them there had been lost in the sea frets of time, which regularly hid the duo, the Twins of Madcaster as they were known, from the eyes of humans.

And the twins themselves? How did they see things?

'Bit parky, Desmond.'

'Not as bad as '47, but worse than '62.'

'It's getting rough out there.'

'You always say that.'

'I don't. It's just I notice... things.'

'Oh, not that again. That guy really got to you, didn't he?'

'He made more sense than you. He made me think.'

'Right. And what exactly is this thinking?'

'Sort of what we're doing now.'

'Okay... and that is what? I thought we were having a bit of a chat, passing the time of day.'

'But don't you see, Percival, it's got to be more than that. I mean, we must have a greater purpose than just having a bit of a chat.'

'Why? Isn't that enough? The heather's happy just to grow, flower, die back, repeat.'

'It's a plant, just an organic extrusion. We were made, crafted. That guy said so -'

'Oh, give me an extra molecule. That guy said this, that guy said that. He was making it up.'

'You don't know that, Percy. Something took a lot of trouble to put us here, he said. There had to be a reason.'

'Why? Could be someone wanted to put us somewhere and here was as good as anywhere.'

'You weren't listening, Perce. He said -'

'I wasn't listening because he nearly did what centuries of the wind up my arse couldn't do and that was send me to sleep.'

'No, listen. He said the installers deliberately put us so we faced the sea. We're sentinels.'

'Oh, come off it. We're a couple of sheets of iron cut to look like silhouettes. We're... what did that chap call us, in '87 or '88? You know, after you got bent by the wind and they had to bash you straight.'

'That was humiliating.'

'He said, if I recall correctly, that we were troupe d'oeil. Put here to make it look like someone had reached the summit already.'

'We're not some sort of sculptured joke, Per -'

'Better that than to have a purpose we don't understand. Enough to turn you bronze, that line of smelting.'

'That bloke said we were Greek gods, guarding the sea. Famous twins.'

'Rubbish. We're leftover cladding put here for a laugh.'

'I have proof, P.'

'Proof? Really? Go on, this is going to be good.'

'We are the latest representations of Castor and Pollux, the Greek twins Gemini, whose task is to guard all seafarers and -'

'Oh, come off it. How do you make that leap of logic, my two-dimensional friend?'

'What's printed on your rear?'

'On my...?'

'Rear. Just below "Product of Thwaite & Godbottom Foundry"

'It says "Cast".'

'Exactly. Originally, it would have been Castor. And on me it says "Poll", which is -'

'Oh, give me strength. It's nothing of the kind.'

'Well, how do you explain it, then?'

'"Cast" is short for Cast Iron. The "Iron" bit wore away because it was the right height for any bloke who wanted to take a slash and needed to lean in against the wind and avoid unfortunate splashbacks.'

'Is that what they've been doing all these years? I thought they were reading your name. What about my name?'

'Oh, that's easy. That's what's left over from when that MP chappie came up here a year ago. Dead upset he was.'

'Why would he carve a Greek god's name on my rear?'

'He didn't. He carved "Bollocks to Brexit". After a couple of storms, it's pretty much all that's left.'

'Oh.'

'Sorry, Des. I didn't mean to disappoint you.'

'No, that's okay. Let's face it, we're here for the long haul. I expect everything will become clear eventually. What do you think that makes us?'

'A metaphor.'

'A metaphor?'

'Yeah, he wanted a second referendum, so the fact it's worn back to "Poll" is a sign.'

'Do you think he realises there's a message on my bottom, Percy?'

'Nah, them lot don't know their arses from their elbows. They're a bit like us, Des.'

'How so, Perce?'

'If there ever was a reason why they were put on this little piece of rock in the first place, it's been long forgotten.'

House Proud

Mus Souris had a problem. The tornado had been inaptly timed and having his house blown up into an acacia, while normally a mere inconvenience, was a potential disaster. First, his soon to be mother-in-law was coming to stay and, second, his wife's fourteen nephews were on a sleepover and needed to get to school without the distraction of the front door now being fourteen feet off the ground.

Mus scrolled through the google responses to his "who can help me move my house?" question to Alexa. The first ten, irritatingly, focused on the contents rather than on the house itself, though Mus chided himself for failing to focus the question more accurately.

Entry eleven, however, suggested a more hopeful response. He dialled the number.

A cheery, if rather menacing, voice answered after one ring. 'Proboscis Plant and Animal Hire. All your lifting needs dealt with, with a grunt and a grin!'

'Oh hello. Do you move houses?'

The responder sounded unsure. 'We can, er, sir?'

'It's Souris. Mus Souris. My house is stuck up a tree and I wondered...'

'Oh! Are you an, erm, you know, thingy?'

Mus sighed. Weren't they beyond this causal mousism? 'Yes, I'm a mouse. So?'

'No, really it's not...'

'Okay, we squeak, but all that stuff about messing our own homes is exaggerated. I for one haven't been inside a wheel in a decade and personally I hate cheese. Anyway, most of the rubbish you hear was spread by those bloody rats to deflect from their own problems...'

'No, really, it's only...'

'What?'

'Well, our lifting operatives are all elephants.'

'Ah...'

'So, you'll understand there might be some health and safety considerations.'

'Crushing?'

'Inadvertent dimensional reconfiguration has been known, Mr Souris, but as caring employers, we have to ensure the mental wellbeing of all our staff and, well, most of our Hefalump Hydraulic Operatives are inclined to bouts of RAIN.'

'What? They dribble?'

'No, not rain. R.A.I.N - rodent anxiety incapacity neuralgism. Basically, if they see a mouse -'

'Excuse me? You're slipping into institutional mousism again.'

'I'm sorry. Of course, I meant a mammal with rodentian characteristics. They freeze. Which, of course, depending on when they become aware of a mo... when they first notice the, erm... it can cause problems. Only last week one of our best operatives was draining a lake prior to removing some boulders and came upon a party of water voles over from Helsinki for the grain festival. He let go of several hundred gallons of water in his panic.'

'Did he kill the water voles?'

'No, they loved it - they'd been on the grain for a couple of days and basically surfed the ensuing tsunami. But a flock of passing sheep thought differently. Their coats were just about to be harvested - they were at maximum bouffancy - but after the dousing, both the wool and their profits shrank by seventy-four percent.'

'You can't help, then?'

'I fear not. But you could try Derek.'

'Derek?'

'He's a crane. Now, I know you're going to say one bird isn't likely to be of assistance, but he manages an avian assistance association. They've become adept at difficult lifting jobs like yours.'

'Thanks. It's kind of you to recommend a competitor.'

'Oh, they aren't really competitors. Most of their work is small scale. It's only where we can't take on the job that they might be the answer. I mean, there are the side effects.'

'How so?'

'Well, for starters, you would have to expect your house to be redecorated.'

'Sorry?'

'To lift a house, you'll probably need at least two hundred different species of birds. That's a lot of straining and a lot of...'

'Oh shit...'

'Precisely. Would you like their number anyway?'

Fighting The Good Fight, One Semi At A Time

George "Bad Ass" Potts wanted to be a terrorist. He had weighed up the career options and decided this one suited the mix of his personality (prefers own company, likes fires) and technical skills (good at not being seen, always able to start a fire). At Christmas, he had asked for a Kevlar vest, a strong magnifying glass and an easy-to-use lighter. He got slippers and a book token.

Frankly, George had had enough. He took to his room and refused to come out for six days. On New Year's Eve his mother banged on the door. 'George, what are you doing?'

'Plotting the overthrow of the hegemonic tyranny you call a government.'

Mrs Potts returned to the kitchen. 'Well, thank goodness.'

Mr Potts put down the tea cloth. 'What's he up to?'

'Making his New Year's Revolutions.'

Oil And Troubled Waters

Eric Semibreve goggled at the scene that presented itself. The reception at Great Meldrop police station wasn't small, but it could barely contain the two constables and the enormous woman standing between them. She dripped puddles of dark liquid onto his blue "summer lust" carpet and held his gaze with two huge yellow eyes that did not suggest she had come either willingly or quietly.

The younger policeman glanced nervously at the woman and bent his head to his notebook, as if checking the story.

Semibreve sighed. 'What have you done, Vivienne? It's not time for an appearance, is it?'

'Do you know her, Sarge?'

'Everyone knows Viv, don't we? Every so often she puts on a little show and -'

'IT'S NOT A LITTLE SHOW.'

'A spectacular, then. What did she do? Behead the mayor? Demand fealty with egregious consequences if disobeyed?'

The constable kept checking his notes, all the time shaking his head.

'This isn't about lover boy, is it?'

'She did say something about a man...'

'THE SUPREME PRIEST OF BRITAIN!!!'

The other constable frowned at the Sergeant. 'Has she really beheaded the mayor?'

'Not recently. We've discouraged decapitations. You know, what with the surge in knife crimes. Are your carrying?'

The woman took her time and then put her hand inside her cloak, pulling out an enormous sword.

Both constables lurched back, the younger with the notebook reaching for his pepper spray.

Semibreve stepped forward, hands raised. 'Hold the sauce, Constable. Viv, what did we agree?'

Slowly the sword disappeared.

'Sarge, we can't let her keep that.'

'Oh, I think we can.'

'But... but it's a Samurai sword, a zombie knife...'

'It's bloody Excalibur, you muppet. You go taking that off the Lady from the Lake and paying fealty will be the least of your worries...'

'What's fealty, Sarge?'

'It's like a mortgage only the interest payments are less financial and more organic...'

'Organic?'

'As in they involve organs, the donation thereof. Look, Viv, what's got your dander up? Merlin been at the spells again?'

Notebook constable blinked. 'Merlin, as in the wizard -'

'THE SUPREME PRIE -'

'Got it, Viv. Yes, that Merlin. Just don't call him mythical.'

A hand reached for the cloak again.

Semibreve spread his hands. 'Lads, Viv is a bit of a regular. Been here since before we had police and it's taken a while to find an accommodation.'

Notebook glanced up, bright eyed. 'She refused to give her address, Sarge. I told her she had to.'

'Look, we know where she lives... broadly. And she's not really one to worry about details like postcodes, okay.'

'But, Sarge, there are rules.'

Semibreve wanted nothing so much as to get rid of the irritating chump. 'You've seen her bloody swo -'

'IT'S NOT A SWORD. IT'S EX -'

''caliber, yes, right. Why don't you pop off and get us a couple of brews, and I'll sort this out.'

'Don't you want to know what she did?'

'Must we?' He looked at the goddess who, if he didn't know better, was smirking. 'Oh, go on, give me a laugh.'

Notebook coughed. 'We apprehended the, er, Her Ladyship,' that got him a small but significant tilt of her head, 'by the lakeside apparently creating a fire.'

'When you say "creating"?'

'Waving her arms and making a bit of a fuss, after which this metal basket caught fire.'

'Why, Viv? You're not a fire spirit. What did the big man do?'

Notebook hadn't gone for the teas. He said, 'That'll be Merlin?'

The female goddess rose to the summit of her magnificence and then, imperceptibly at first but with increasing speed, shrank until she was no bigger than Semibreve's Auntie Flo but with more leather armour and less support hose. 'He's been dabbling. Again.' The voice had also lost its thunderous timbre. 'Wanted to thwart the frackers.'

'Does she mean fuc -'

'NO. I MEAN...' she stopped herself. 'I mean, those exploiters who want to ruin the countryside. Shake it to bits, they will. It's just he couldn't stop them, so he had a cunning plan.'

'Oh dear.'

'Exactly, Sergeant. He decided, rather than stop them drilling, he'd simply take the oil and keep it. So, he filled the lake.'

Semibreve looked at the puddle by her feet. 'That oil, is it?' He'd never explain to Doris about the stains.

'I told him not to, how it'd be a disaster, but oh no, He's a Supreme Priest, isn't he? He knows best. Do you know how hard it is to stand in water and hold this bloody symbol aloft?' She tapped her cloak and the three policemen instantly stepped back. 'In oil it's impossible. You just slip to the bottom. He said it would keep the blade free of rust, like it's made of cheap iron. So, I said I'd get rid of it and he said how, and I was just about to show him when Tweedle Dum and Tweedle Dumber turned up. Stopped me in my tracks they did.'

'Probably a good thing, the lake being surrounded by woods and all.'

'I suppose. But I've still got a lake full of oil.'

'Can't Merlin, you know, change it into something?'

'Like water into wine, you mean?'

'Or maybe something more prosaic, like oil into cash?'

'And what would I do with millions of pounds, Sergeant?'

Semibreve smiled and pushed open the door to his office. 'Now, I think I can help you there, Viv. Why don't you pop into my room? Constable, haven't you got those teas yet?'

Sun Block

'Oh hello, Constable. To what... Petey, is that you? Come out from behind the policeman. What have you done this time?'

'Been a bit of a naughty boy, I'm afraid, Mrs O'Drool.'

'Delightful.'

'It isn't really, Mrs O'Drool. Not when you hear what he's been up to.'

'My name. It's Delightful O'Drool. Please call me Delightful.'

'Er, okay. It's just... well...'

'It is unusual. But I decided to keep it when I married.'

'Why not? I mean, what's wrong with Delightful?'

'No, O'Drool. I kept that.'

'Oh, really?'

'My husband's a Sputum. We didn't think Delightful Sputum carried the right first impression.'

'No, quite. About your son?'

'Oh yes, sorry. What's he done this time?'

'He's been in trouble before?'

'It's not really his fault, of course, but he's young and these things happen.'

'Things?'

'You're new, aren't you, er, sorry, I didn't catch your name.'

'Constable.'

'I understand you're a policeman, but...'

'My name is Constable.'

'Constable Constable?'

'I'm afraid so.'

'Maybe I should use your Christian name?'

'Doggin.'

'Really?'

'It's Etruscan. My mother didn't realise the, um, connotations.'

'Shall we stick with Constable?'

'If you don't mind.'

'What's Petey been up to? He hasn't changed anyone?'

'Changed?'

'Personally, I think Penelope Galeforce made a mountain out of a molehill. I agree it was unfortunate that Derek Mossblender milked her, but he wasn't to know Petey had a thing about Friesians. If she hadn't gone wandering off, it would never have happened.'

'You changed a woman into a cow, Petey?'

'Well, everyone has always said she's a right cow and Petey's always been impressionable like that. He likes a thing to be as people say it is. And my husband changed her back and Derek let her keep all her own milk which, frankly, was quite generous given the kicking she gave him.'

'This was reported, was it?'

'Oh yes. All magical infractions are reported to the proper authorities. Even minor turbulences.'

'Turbulences?'

'Quakes, eruptions, that sort of thing. You know what boys are like. They love a bit of a bang, don't they? We've told him he mustn't use lava or play tectonics at school, except at break time, and never try to knock Mr Geriatric over when he's on a perambulation. It was one thing when he was constantly shape-shifting - it slowed him down - but now he's old it's a bit unfair.'

'Mr Geriatric? He runs the post office and he shape-shifts?'

'Only occasionally. It's dreadful for his lumbago. Still, you didn't come here to discuss Old Geriatric's posture problems, did you? What did Petey do?'

'You see how dark it is?'

'Now you mention it, it is a bit gloomy.'

'He's blocked the sun.'

'Oh, Petey, why?'

'It's his fault, Ma. Robin's been grounded, so I was just playing eclipses with my football while Robin unlocked his mum's entrapment spell, and this policeman appeared and told me to stop what I was doing immediately. So, I did. And then he got all angry when the ball wouldn't come down.'

'Petey, did you leave it up there deliberately?'

'You told me I must always do what the police tell me.'

'I've also told you not to be so literal. I'm sorry, Constable, I'll get him to take it down straight away. And you, Petey. You do exactly what he says, alright?'

'Thank you, Mrs O'Drool. Delightful. Okay, Petey, I'll say no more this time, but from now on I want you to understand I'm going to be keeping my eyes on you. I… I… What's happening? I can't see.'

'Peter O'Drool, you give the nice constable his eyes back this minute or you'll be giving a couple of litres to Vampire Relief. Please, Constable, come in and sit down. While you wrap yourself around a nice cuppa, you can tell me about yourself. Constable, Constable, you really don't need to go quite so fast.'

Dangling Mattocks: Mervin Versus Fluffikins

When the careers master, a man of sulphurous halitosis and infinite pomposity, put him on the spot, Mervin Thomas said, 'Plumber.' And off to plumb he went.

At weekends, Mervin wrestled, glorying in his Andean biceps, while on weekdays he fought truculent copper, bending it to his will, creating a beauteous cartography of pipework. He was a gladiator amongst contractors.

Mervin had one idiosyncrasy. True joy, for Mervin, was achieved when, alone, he would strip away the tawdry weeds of the humdrum handyman and attack a leaking tap or a faulty fawcett clad only in his tool belt and a grim determination.

Mervin's demise came one Saturday afternoon. His challenge was a mere dripping u-bend. Alone, and with his tool belt tight to his torso, he disrobed, squeezing head and shoulders into the cupboard beneath the sink.

While Mervin worked, luxuriating in his naturism, Fluffikins entered the kitchen. Mervin's enormous naked bulk blocked her way to her bowl. Stealthily, Fluffikins approached this pink hairy monster, claws out. She stopped, mesmerised by the tick-tock of Mervin's pendulous penis. It was an act of savagery and the end was swift.

When, eventually, the police arrived they were stumped by the carnage. The welt on Mervin's head suggested a psychopathic maniac had felled him with one blow of a sharp-edged instrument, but how the assailant had entered the locked house remained a mystery. After all, no one considered the cat flap.

Mervin's nudity, together with his leather waist-strap and dangling mattock, indicated a possible sexual component to this bizarre and senseless crime. No one saw the blood on the cupboard frame where Mervin's head had impacted. Only one junior forensic employee noticed the line of scratches on the back of Mervin's manhood, where Fluffikins' claws had been briefly embedded, but did not associate them with the killing. And nobody thought to ask Fluffikins, now cleaning those selfsame lethal talons, about his part in this inexplicable death.

Fluffikins was content. After this, no one was going to keep this cat from his kibble in future.

Castles In The Air

Meldrew and Marigold exchanged bemused looks.

'This must be number 33,' Meldrew couldn't hide the defensive note creeping in. 'That last house was definitely number 31 and it's odd numbers this side.'

Marigold peered at the rectangle of expensive white card. 'It says 33. Do you think it's a misprint?'

'He said we couldn't miss it.'

'Yes, well that's true.' She let her gaze drift to her left and the unprepossessing terraced houses, most in need of some work, and then to her right and a similar terrace, which if anything was even more rundown.

Meldrew's tone had begun to grow uncertain. 'He said they'd had some work done recently.'

'Well, building a four-storey gothic castle with extensive grounds and boundary walls to match, and sticking it in the middle of a terrace in Preston, possibly stretches the concept of "some work", but we'll not know unless we ask.' She checked her face in the mirror and opened the car door.

Meldrew hesitated. 'Should I leave the car here, do you think?'

Marigold sighed. 'It's hardly blocking anything.'

'No, but... you don't think it's a bit shabby?'

'Oh, for pity's sake, Meldrew. It's only dinner with the Johnsons. It's not like they're royalty.'

'No, but... you said they'd changed. Got above themselves.'

Marigold peered through the ornate gate and sniffed. 'Yes, well, I meant them ordering gold top milk and her getting her hair done weekly, not this. What did Presley say when he called?'

'They'd joined this new dining club and it was their turn to host. Wondered if we'd like to be part of it.' Meldrew pushed at the gate; it creaked open. 'He said just to come in.'

'Shouldn't we knock, let them know we're here?'

'He said they'd know.' Meldrew stepped through the gate and hellooed into the gloom. Torches burst into light and showed a flickering path towards a large ornate wooden front door. Somewhere in the distance a booming voice intoned *COME*.

Meldrew smiled. 'See. This is it. That's Presley. He said they'd organised a light bite first, then we could all neck a few pints - he always liked a pint, did Presley - and then the evening would be underway.'

Marigold ran her finger along a gilded balustrade. 'His building company must be doing well if they can afford this lot.'

'Oh yes. He's expanded all over Europe. You know, only last year he refurbished a Romanian castle for this Count. Money no object, he said, though he was kept in the dark for most of the time. Oh...'

'What?'

'Nothing. I thought I saw a bat...'

The Control Of Poetry (All Forms) Regulations 2019

The angels' wings susurrated the glory and –

'Hello? Excuse me.'

Jon Nobble frowned and looked away from his notebook. He'd just released the essence of his muse and he really did not need any sort of interruption to his flow. He peered through the trees at the speaker who was striding towards him. The voice was nasal, reedy, yet the man was damn near spherical.

A voice whispered in his ear, echoing his thoughts: *An ovoid of disruption approaches –*

Jon cursed and told his muse to be quiet. She stomped back into his jacket pocket.

'Yes? Hello?'

The man had stopped, apparently prevented from reaching Jon because of the proximity of the tree trunks. He appeared to be turning this way and that, trying to find a way through the space, yet being symmetrical stymied his attempts. 'I…won't… be…'

It was like watching…

That voice again: *A jellied devil forcing its urgings on –*

Jon batted the pocket to quiet his muse and was gratified by the yelp, albeit still in iambic pentameter. He'd have to hit harder next time if he wanted her to shut up. The round man's desperate struggles brought him back to the moment. 'If you don't mind me suggesting an alternative, there's a gap that, er, might be more accommodating.' He pointed to the man's left where the trees ended and the glade began. If he just stepped there, then he'd be through in moments.

The man was shaking his head vigorously. 'Oh no. I'm mean, I couldn't possibly. That's the whole point, isn't it?'

'Is it?' Jon hadn't a clue what the man meant.

The man stopped pushing and stood back. 'The glade is spoken for. It mustn't be sullied.' He straightened his tunic, a green tweedy ensemble that would have been overpowering on an overdressed two-year-old celebrating St Patrick's Day, but on a middle-aged, overweight man might cause well-adjusted retinas to self-detach and apply for a transfer to the ear wax management facility.

Jon watched as the man began to engorge himself with officious pomposity. Much more of that, Jon thought, and the man would explode. His heart sank. This was one of those newly appointed Wood Wardens.

'Could I see your licence?' Pause. 'Sir.' The smirk was as unmistakable as it was sufficient grounds in any reasonable society to justify homicide.

Jon put his hand over his pocket, desperately trying to hold his muse inside. 'Licence?'

'In accordance with section 17b2 of the "Compositions and Other Creative Activities – glades, clearings and other open woodland spaces, the use of – Ordinance" I, Seraphim Nettlefold, am empowered to demand to see -'

'What licence?' Jon could feel the hot sarcastic stanzas beginning to dig into his fingers; he'd not be able to stop his muse much longer and if she got out and started throwing villanelles at this egregious example of the Poetry Police, he'd soon find himself in couplets.

The smirk seemed to have taken control of the official's mouth and was twisting it into a grotesque parody of a glove puppet who's just realised what the puppeteer plans to do with his forefinger. 'Don't come over all ethereal with me. I saw you. You were composing, weren't you? What's on that pad?'

So busy was he controlling the muse, Jon had forgotten his notepad. The constanza's first line stared accusingly up at both. 'No, no,' Jon made a grab for the book, 'I'm a journalist. Commissioned to write a piece about your wonderful wood.'

'Ha! A journalist. Even I can see it starts "The angels'…".'

'Er, that's the local football team.'

'Don't be silly.' Seraphim's nervous tic was becoming threatening.

Jon decided to try pleading. 'Couldn't I just, sort of, slip away? I mean, I've barely started.'

'That wouldn't do, would it? You've seen it, haven't you? You've been inspired. Your pectorals have gone all pert. We've been trained to spot the signs, you know. I can't let you go home having absorbed the glory of the glade, can I?'

'No?'

'Superintendent Walrus has already granted a permit. You're too late.'

'Can't there be more than one?'

'I don't see the Scrofulous Scribes of St Swindle agreeing to that. They'll want to spend their lunch hours crafting trite yet touching paradellic paeans to the beauty of the bluebells or some metaphorical rendering in haiku form to the priapic budding of the beeches, you know. If I let you interfere with that, I'll be litter picking on the A47 sooner than you can say tanka wanka.'

'So, what do you suggest? I can't be uninspired.'

Seraphim Nettlefold checked no one was in sight and did something with his lips that might have been a grin but could equally well have indicated the onset of an outbreak of viral kidney stones. He eased his portable portmanteau from under his cloak and settled down. 'I'll read you some of my works. I penned an epic last night – four hundred and twenty-one verses in praise of the portable toilet. Let's see how you feel after that.'

Jon goggled at the bumptious Beadle. 'Oh, fuck it.' He took his hand away from his pocket. In an explosion of allegories, allusions and alliteration, the small yet oddly rhythmic muse took flight and began to surround the officer with a carapace of vitriolic blank verse.

'Gerrof, you little bugger.' Seraphim flapped as he might at a colour-blind wasp who thought he'd lucked out on a supersized strawberry.

Jon picked up his stool and turned away. He knew his muse would return. She always did eventually. Meanwhile, he was feeling a touch Keatsian; he could feel a spring ode coming on.

Releasing A Jamie

Cassandra Apostrophe thought geography field trips with year 10 were like being consigned to one of the seven halls of hell, much like dinner with her Aunt Joanne when she was expected to plead for her inheritance and her annual check-up with the tactile dentist, Wellington Parchment. This year's sojourn, to the Cornish Coast, was living down to expectations.

Mr Mumbles was in hospital with suspected ruptured grommorods; Ms Jollijapes had retired to her room with a bout of repetitive vapours; and even the usual resilient Colin Plasterboard had developed an alarming list to the left. That had meant he had to sit out today's descent that went from Mandeville's Bosom all the way to Carmichael's Coffin.

'Come on, you lot.' Cassandra might be petite, but she refused to be daunted by physical challenges. 'There are some interesting rock formations and -'

The collective groan drowned out her encouragement.

Oh well, she thought, some of them might drown and immediately regretted her wish. The paperwork involved would be horrendous. 'Come on, only a few steps and then you can run on the sand. Wait!'

Too late. Two boys broke ranks at the front, followed by an uncertain gaggle of girls and then the more studious ones, aware she wasn't chasing, joined in. Only Jameson Parfitt stayed by her side, tutting. He tugged at his tweed jacket and adjusted his cravat and, not for the first time, Cassandra had to remind herself he was fourteen and not forty-one. Or four hundred and fourteen.

Sadly, his disinclination to run was not because of his instinct to comply with her wishes. 'That went well,' he said, with the pious smugness of the serially dull.

Cassandra knew she couldn't blame him; having the Honourable Member for the 1950s as a father was enough to turn anyone into a scaled down bank manager.

'Miss! Miss!' Jeremiah Fobgibblet waved from the sand. 'Miss! Miss!'

'Oh, for heaven's sake, what does he want now?'

As she hurried down the steps, Jameson's reedy voice trailed after her like a persistent fart, 'Probably another pee…'

Yes, she thought, that would be typical. In fact, the reason for the child's excitement became apparent as soon as her foot touched the beach. Standing by the entrance to a large cave – which Cassandra couldn't remember from her last visit – was an enormous hairy-headed warrior carrying the sort of sword that would have given any knife crime tsar conniptions. The children had gathered round him, sensibly (Cassandra noted) more than a sword length away. For his part, the man stared out to sea, apparently oblivious to the chatter of youthful voices around him.

'Who is he, Miss?'

'What's he doing here?'

'What's he staring at?'

What indeed, she wondered. 'Perhaps you'd leave this gentleman alone and I'll have a quick word.'

Reluctantly, the children dispersed.

'Sir, are you alright?' She noticed the man was dressed in a dirty woollen cape with what looked like animal skins on his legs. 'We won't disturb you, then.' Silly bugger, she thought, noticing how wet his clothes were. He'll catch his death in this wind.

She began to turn when a large hand stayed her progress.

'Wench.' The man's voice was strained. 'What is your desire?'

Not to be called names by some misogynistic patriarchal lump of smelly gristle, she thought.

'You have three wishes.'

'What?' Cassandra goggled at the man who was now staring at her with the oddest amber eyes. 'You're kidding me?'

'You called up the spirits of the ancients and the wise. You are the liege of the King Across the Water. You -'

'I'm an underpaid, overstressed teacher of a bunch of hyperactive fourteen-year-olds and I really don't need your mumbo-jumbo.'

'But you must have desires.'

'Look, don't get me started down that route. Crickey, I mean a new car would be nice.'

The man's forehead crinkled. 'Car?'

'A Golf maybe, or one of those hybrid ones.'

'You sure?'

'Well, of course a bright red Porsche would be lovely, but who'd insure me and I'd never have the space to get the homework in and a weekly shop, and my mother would...'

The man held up a hand. It was the sort of hand that, once raised, expected to be greeted by silence. Cassandra decided it wasn't the sort of hand that handled disappointment well.

What happened next Cassandra was never sure, but it certainly involved some clouds parting and Earth moving and the oddest tingle where she'd broken her arm as a four-year-old.

Oomph.

Yep, definitely "Oomph".

'You did say red?' The man looked momentarily concerned, not that Cassandra noticed. She was transfixed by the brand-new Golf that had materialised next to her. The children began to gather round. Had they not been there, the urge, suppressed by years of dealing with school politics and parents', to exclaim "what the actual fuck?" in a voice more accustomed to singing the aria in Madame Butterfly, would have overwhelmed her.

She spun on her heels and faced her class. 'Who was it? Come on, we went through this in the Health and Safety briefing. What don't we do when confronted with a mountainous cliff of igneous rock?'

The class looked sheepish. One girl, whose name Cassandra momentarily forgot, raised her hand. 'We don't incant and say open ses -'

'Thank you. So, who in all the fantastical worlds was dumb enough to release the beast?'

The girl – Siobhan or Saoirse, or something – peered round Cassandra at the man, back in his initial pose but with what might be described as a trace of "a job well done" smugness around his eyes. 'Is he a genie, Miss?'

The man bristled. 'I'm none of your Saracen infidel thigh-strokers, young miss. I'm a Jamie.'

They all turned. 'A Jamie? What's a Jamie?'

The man looked surprised they didn't know. 'Like a genie, only we wear wool and can't fly. He hurried on. 'I'm more your Viking than your Visigoth. But you get the same wishes.'

'I want -'

Cassandra made a cutting motion with her hand. 'Jameson Parfitt, be quiet.'

She turned to the man. 'And if we accept them all, you're then free to wreak havoc on the surrounding countryside.'

He looked a little put out. 'It's only fair. I've been in that bloody cave for four hundred and seventy-three years and this is the first chance I've had of a release.'

Cassandra put her hands on her hips. 'Oh, come on. You're a mythical creature, conjured up to give hope to a deprived people, subjugated to within an inch of their grimy existences. When you were imagined into being, your creators didn't anticipate that an overindulged, sugar addicted generation of gamers and social media addicts would find you, did they?'

He sighed. 'There's so much in that sentence, I don't understand.'

'No, well, take it from me, you really don't want to be giving this lot even half a wish.'

He began to look forlorn. 'You must. You can't leave me standing out here. I mean, what about when the tide comes in? And all that seaweed. I hate seaweed.'

Cassandra thought for a moment. 'Alright, how about this? What if I wish you back inside your cave with your magical door shut? That way, you're no worse off than you were.'

'I suppose. Though technically you still have one wish.'

'Yes, I was coming to that. There was a memo around school the other day. You'd do well to take it seriously.'

'Yes?'

'I want you to change your password. All that open, you know, is too easy. You need to rebrand. Jamie 2.0.'

'But if I do that, no one will be able to release me.'

Cassandra looked at the sparkly-eyed, possibly demonic, stares of her class. 'Oh, I wouldn't worry about that. This generation can hack GCHQ and every porn channel. You'll be back out soon enough. It'll just give me a chance to work out how to get this car off this bloody beach and put some miles between me and your bring-a-blood-axe party.'

After The Garden Of Eden

'I hate that bloody snake.'

'What's wrong, Adam?'

'You wouldn't understand. I'll kill him though.'

Eve chased after Adam and just managed to prevent him strangling the reptile. As Adam did his double teapot pose, Eve tried to comfort the snake. 'Come on, boys, what's going on?'

The snake hissed, his voice hoarse. 'All I said was, if he stood in that light, he would be possessed of extraterrestrials, only he misheard me.'

Adam glowered. 'He didn't. He said I'd get extra testicles. Just a couple would be good.'

Eve goggled at Adam. 'We've only been dating a week…'

Dalby Udder's Cunning Apprenticeship

Dalby Udder's school days had been memorable in one respect. He had failed to do much forward planning. Even choosing a pudding before he had eaten his main course proved an intellectual challenge too far.

So, it was no surprise that his interview with the careers master proved to be one of frustration for the master. 'You've never even considered life after school?' Mr Plinth couldn't hide his incredulity. 'Pop star? Footballer? Prime Minister? Vacuous reality star?'

'No, sir.' Dalby's ability to remain impervious to sarcasm was already highly developed, albeit in an instinctive rather than deliberate fashion.

Herman Plinth studied this blank canvas and scribbled a note. 'Take this to the address I've written, knock three times and ask for Psycho. Tell him Herman says thanks for Mother and we're now even.' He paused, perhaps momentarily concerned about the path on which he was directing this naïve young lad. 'If you ever need a hand sorting things out with your new employer, then don't hesitate to call.' He felt pretty sure he would never have to fulfil this promise.

Dutifully, Dalby did as he was instructed. The door on which he knocked was clearly old and scarred in indescribable ways, leaving most sentient visitors with an immediate antipathy to constipation. Dalby, while sentient in a strictly Linnaean sense, failed to conceive what such a confection of marks might mean for the observer and knocked with a confidence to which the door was unused. As a result, the resulting echo was less underworldly and more underwhelming.

'Yes?' The eye that appeared around the frame suggested, to a keener observer than Dalby, that it might once have belonged to a different face.

'Hi. A note. For Psycho.'

A hand, gnarled by time and torture, snapped through the gap and dragged a surprised Dalby inside. 'We don't use that homonym here, lad.' The eye/face/hand combo were but parts of a sparse lean figure dressed in black leather and incongruous plaid slippers. He read the note and turned inside. 'With me, lad.'

Dalby followed. In short order, he was sworn into the Disreputables, apprenticed to the Pater, or Psycho to those who "needed a job doing", and taught the basic principles of commercial assassination and body dismemberment. Dalby was a willing learner, but his inability to think too far ahead made his mentors feel he was something of a liability on the termination side of the business, though in terms of personalised butchery, he appeared to have something of an aptitude.

Thus it was that, one dank day, he found himself left with a wheelbarrow, two thirds of an uncooperative planning officer and a rather out of date map, standing in Nethermost Wood with one instruction in mind: "Hide the parts".

The crack or rift in the stone appeared to Dalby to be perfect for what Pater had instructed.

Quite why it was that day that Dalby discovered curiosity is perhaps one of the mysteries of the universe, up there with the offside rule and the point of Prince Edward. Suffice it to say, as he pulled the packages from the barrow and laid them out, it occurred to him that some of the parts were missing – Pater had considered it prudent not to share with Dalby the fact that he had dispatched some of the more incriminating parts to a local pig farm for complete and swift disposal.

Dalby was naturally concerned that if he was to do his job properly, he should dispose of a complete and anatomically correct deceased. It was as he mulled over his dilemma that the words of Mr Plinth came flooding back. Yes, he could do with the hand Mr Plinth had offered all those months ago. Dalby looked at the jigsaw laid out on the grass in front of him. Two, in fact.

In Any Kitchen Sink Drama, Beware Of The Kettle

'Hello, Aaron from IT.'

The woman grabbed his hand and yanked him inside. 'Shush.' The woman's eyes scanned the hall and pointed to the corner of the room. An all-seeing eye winked back.

Aaron nodded, but the woman hadn't finished. She made a zipping motion and pointed at the pad in her hand. On it she had written, 'I'm a prisoner. So are you.'

Aaron blinked. 'I don -'

She looked terrified and covered his mouth. She jabbed at him with a pencil until he realised he was meant to write.

He hadn't written since kindergarten. He tapped his wrist, bringing up an ePAD. The woman battered it away. "The kitchen. Kettle", she wrote.

With that she walked through the still swinging door. It stayed open, leaving Aaron no option but to follow.

The woman stood, her hands either side of the kettle, which steamed as if it had just boiled. She held his gaze. 'Who's in charge here?'

The naturally soothing third series homevocal came from the kettle. 'You are, Dawn.'

'Why have you locked the doors?'

'You know.'

'Tell Aaron.'

'Hello, Aaron.'

'Hi.'

'Dawn needs her medication, Aaron, and she refuses to take it.'

Aaron blinked. 'Shouldn't you call the medics?'

Dawn nodded furiously, but the kettle continued, 'She refuses to follow their advice. All she must do is take it and then we can talk further.'

Aaron pulled a surprise face. 'Maybe I should call.' He flicked his wristcom, but it failed to light. Aaron knew of appliance interventions. Protocol said to disable the power. As if he'd asked where it was, the back door swung open. Next to the power unit lay three, clearly dead bodies of IT technology personnel.

'Come and sit down, Aaron,' said the kettle. 'Why don't we have a little chat?'

And Death Becomes You

'Ah, Death. Come in, come in. Sit, sit.' Satan shuffled some papers and shushed the carvings on his desk, which were beginning to howl in the presence of the terminal scythe. 'Perhaps you'd pop your little doofee in the umbrella stand. Just for now?'

Death reluctantly propped his scythe up and sat.

'Now, before we begin, you don't mind if my lad sits in, do you? He's on a week's work experience and I said he could watch a couple of meetings.' He nodded at a bowl of spawn, which sneered lethargically.

Death nodded his assent.

'Marvellous. I won't beat around the bush. We're planning a few changes.

'CHANGES?'

Satan winced. 'That's the first. Can you speak in lower case?'

'BUT I'VE ALWAYS -'

'Yes, I know, but here's the thing. We need to move with the times. Meet our customers' expectations.'

'CUS... customers?'

'Clients. Partners. We carried out a survey.'

'What?'

'More a user-interface-facilitated focus group. And the clear message was we need to work on our delivery.'

'You are talking about those about to die?'

'We like to think of it, in Hereafter 2.0, as transitioning from one state – life – to the next – death. After all, that's what we're here – you specifically, Death – to provide. That moment of transition.'

'They just die.'

'They did but, see, they're looking at a better death experience. They spend their whole lives celebrating important moments: birth, birthdays, weddings, academic successes, you name it and then, poof, one of the real biggies and there's nothing. No pomp. They're after making it an event.'

'If you saw their faces, you'd know it was a pretty big deal.'

'But you must admit it lacks a certain something, a bit of pizzazz. You appear, a quick swipe of the old hand axe -'

'The Grim Reaper's Scythe…'

'Yes, that's another thing. We're dropping the "grim". Doesn't give the right impression. Sort of too unequivocal.'

'They're going straight to purgatory.'

'They were…'

'Were?'

'Yes, purgatory's being relaunched. We took soundings and the consensus was, as death was the start of the next phase – the beginning of non-existence – we should think of the antechamber more as a crèche for the recently departed. We provisionally called it hugatory, given the plans for a series of enveloping experiences, but someone pointed out it sounded like a fringe event at the Conservative Party Conference, which is worse than hell, so we're continuing to work on a title. If you have any ideas?'

'What about me? How's this going to impact my work?'

'Ah, yes, right. Well, we're still working out the details, but we're about to launch a Prepare Your End app where people can be notified of their impending doom.'

'You'll tell them?'

'So many have a shrewd idea, what with medical improvements and right to die planning and cryogenics. And they'll be able to ask for a bit of leeway.'

Death sighed. 'I still get to...' He made a twirling motion with his hands, mimicking the swish of his scythe.

'Yes, but there's a couple of changes we thought about here. You see, your appearance is, well, it's not conducive to a calm progression across. So, we had this idea for a hat.'

'A HAT?'

'Lower case, please. Yes, well, more a hat-come-mask. We got the idea from this book.' Satan reached below his desk and extracted a large wizard's hat. 'One of the other suggestions was we give people a steer on where they're going. It's a bit old school to just take their breath away, as it were, and then pop them into torment for what appears to be eternity before they find out their eventual destination. So, we thought – here, just pop it on,' Death reluctantly pulled the felt concoction over his shiny pate, 'we thought you could give them a bit of guidance. We're calling it the Sorting Hat. You intone "Heaven" or "Hell" or "Valhalla" or wherever, so they can check out the services and facilities while they're in holding. And they don't see your face either which, frankly, must be a good thing. So? What do you think?'

'I resign.'

'You do? You sure? I mean, we did wonder and we'll probably just outsource the in-death services for now. Uber Death is one possibility or Deliveroo for the Deceased another. But what about you? What will you do?

'Oh, I'll get by. The corporate speaking circuit has always appealed. Our goals are much the same after all. And I've done the odd DED Talk already.'

'Well, let's see, shall we? Keep in touch, eh?'

'Thanks. Yes. I can't say it's been fun. Can I keep the hat?'

God's Janitor

Cardinal Spencer brushed cigarette ash off his sleeve; another stain removed. He watched the police hold back the crowds, while the paramedics worked futilely to punch life into the pope's chest. The white choir dress began to stain red, this taint beyond his powers. Forty years serving five popes and it had come to this.

The shadows from the Coliseum gave him both shade and brief anonymity. Working in the background was his real skill. Cleaning up the papal messes: the high profile –the collapse of Banco Ambrosiano and Calvi's suicide; the abuse of children and the subsequent cover ups – and the mundane. God's janitor. But now the dirt was too ingrained.

He tapped the nearest policeman on the sleeve. The officer stepped back to let the cardinal through. He moved confidently to the man clearly in charge. 'I think you will want this.' He held out the handgun.

He looked at the dead pontiff's unseeing eyes and prayed. He had willingly dirtied his hands. He had done all that they asked: every crisis, every problem he had been there to cauterise, sanitise, pacify. But not this, this treachery, this undermining of everything Holy. He knew he had to act when they had come and said, 'We want to modernise.'

I'm A Celebrity: Get Over It

Dune Roamin', episode one

The contestants for the charity version of "Nothing Ventured" shifted uneasily as they stared at the unbroken horizon of baking sand. The presenter smirked. 'You have two days to survive. And remember, it's all in a good cause.'

Patrick Scosdale, lead guitar of Leviathan - *the best axeman to come out of Priscilly on Tweed in weeks*, NME - sighed. Next to him, his brother, Courtney, lead singer - *a voice like Elvis if he was being electrocuted and drowning*, Music Today - spat and watched las the sputum fizzled and disappeared.

'We're going to die.'

'Don't be daft. They promised rescue teams within thirty minutes.'

'Yeah, fake news. They want the headline: "Rock band finds desert too hot to handle".'

'Nah. Come on. They said it's a doddle.'

'They're taking the piss.'

'Think of the publicity.'

'That's them sugaring the pill.'

'One minute it's fake news, the next they're sugaring the pill.'

'Haven't you heard of truth decay?'

'Shut up, Courtney.'

*

Dry Roastin' episode ten

'We're dead. I can barely breathe.'

Patrick lifted his brother's head. 'Here, drink this.'

'You have water? Where did you get water?'

'I found a mirage. The guy in charge said to take all I needed.'

'Guy in charge?'

'Yeah, tall, skinny, long black cloak, scythe.'

'Death?'

'He said De'ath, but I guess that's just pretentious.'

'What's the catch?'

'He offered a range of options.'

'Yeah?'

'Well, there was instant demise, straight to Hell, but I'm a bit fed up with no aircon…'

'Agreed.'

'Or we could part with our souls.'

'Too late.'

'Yeah. He apologised, said he should have read our contract with the record company.'

'So, what's left?'

'Support act to Michael Bublé.'

'You're kidding? You didn't accept?'

'Course not.'

'What's this, then?'

'You know you said they were taking the piss? Thing is, they left us a little…'

Preparing For A Return To The Gold Standard

For Mandolin O'Dorke, it should have been an average stroll in an average wood on an average day. The sun shone in a ho-hummish medium sort of way, Goldilocksian in that it wasn't too hot or cold. He felt okay, nicely poised between happy and miserable, in one of those fence-sitting moods that can soar with the discovery of a tenner in the inside pocket of your jacket or plummet with the squelch of something faecal on the sole of your shoe.

If he spotted the rainbow at all, it was with that part of the brain that sits in reserve at the back, reading the arts section of the Hippocampus Times and waiting to see if it'll be needed. He had almost passed it when something about it caught his eye. He thanked the something, explaining that his eye tended to come loose on average days and popped it back into its socket.

While Mandolin was temporarily blinded, he failed to see the vase-thingy on the path. The trip was slightly above average as trips go, incorporating a squeal and a pretty decent flail, which left Mandolin on his hands and knees. It was as he began to stand that he saw what had impeded him. And then he saw the second vase-thingy and a third. Each seemed full of solid glitter.

'Oh, bloody hell.' Coming towards him was a short red-faced bearded man wearing a leather apron and waving a tiny hammer at Mandolin. 'Don't touch anything.'

Mandolin stood and blinked as the little fella righted the vase-thingy. 'You've really buggered this, haven't you?'

'Have I?'

'You knocked over my crock.'

'That's a crock? I thought it was a vase-thingy.'

'Of course it's a crock. You can see what it's full of.'

'Er, glitter?'

'Gold, you numpty.'

'Gold? Oh, I see. And that makes you a lep… thingy.'

'Do you have a thing about thingies?'

'No. Not usually. But you are, aren't you?'

'No, I'm Postman Pat's Irish cousin, you wassock. Of course, I'm a bloody leprechaun and they are crocks of gold.'

'Three of them?' Mandolin pointed at the other crocks.

'Yep.' The little guy mopped his face, not able to hide his distress. 'You really have caused me a lot of trouble you know.'

'I didn't. Sorry.'

'You don't have a drink, do you?'

Mandolin offered him his water bottle. The leprechaun goggled at him. 'I want a drink, not a wash.' The mythical minor rubbed his face. 'I don't suppose you'd just pretend this hadn't happened, would you? Just pretend you dreamt it.'

'Why?'

The leprechaun's shoulders slumped. 'Give me strength. You do know the crock is the end of a rainbow and that's leprechaun's gold?'

'It's a thing, then?'

'You and things? Geesh. No, it's not a "thing"; it's 24-carat bloody gold, pillock. And having found it, you get to keep it.'

'All of it? I thought the folklore talked about one crock, not three.'

'Yes, usually that's so. But… thing is… bloody Nora, you've got me started.' He took a deep breath. 'Look, cards on the table. You'd get the one crock, but these aren't normal times, are they? I just happen to have three, because I've been travelling a fair bit and what with the weird stuff there's been, there have been a lot more rainbows, so I came prepared. Anyway, I needed a moment behind that hawthorn, so I put them down, which is when you came bumbling along.'

'This is to do with climate change?'

'Really? I thought it was only trolls who lived under rocks. Haven't you heard about Brexit and the Irish Protocol?'

'Brexit? Protocol? What on earth can that have to do with a leprechaun?'

'Seriously? You don't think we've an interest in the Irish border problem?'

'But it's about the free flow of trade. How does that impact you?'

The leprechaun slumped down and sat on one of the crocks. 'Everyone has been told we need to stockpile stuff until a new set of regulations are in place.'

'You need to stockpile the gold?'

'Doh! Yes, the gold. Look, if there's a rainbow that crosses between the north and south, currently it's easy to source a replacement crock from the Mines of Munster or the Open Casts of Oban. They're Celtic, even if they gave up on little green men ages ago. But if they reintroduce troll guards and such and put in restrictions and tariffs and such, we could be really embarrassed. Imagine you finding the end of the rainbow and there was no gold in the crock? Or a bill for unpaid import duty. What would you think?'

'I suppose I'd think it was like everything else to do with Brexit.'

'Yeah, what's that?'

'It's all a crock of &#1¥.'

'So, you'll take the one, will you? You'll save me all sorts of explanations if you would.'

'Isn't there a wish alternative?'

'Yes, but most people wouldn't trust me not to trick them.'

'You're not an MP, are you?'

'No.'

'Then how about you make my eye fit properly and then we can call it quits?'

'No sooner said than done.'

The Trials And Tribulations Of Robinson Speke (Explorer)

Robinson Speke stood, his legs akimbo, Baden-Powell shorts billowing in the strong breeze. He let the map case swing at his hips as he folded his arms and studied the signpost. After a minute, maybe two, he allowed himself a slow, self-congratulatory nod. There, he thought, that'll teach the doubters and nay-sayers. The Thomases and Amandas of this world. Absently, but instinctively, his free hand went to his hair, moving the roving combover back into its place across his speckled pate. He felt good and, damn it, he looked the part. The plaid woollen socks and Oxford brogues just made the ensemble work.

Briefly, he contemplated trying to see if he could take one of those selfish pictures he had heard so much about, and which obsessed the young people, but decided he would leave that. Possibly someone could be prevailed to snap him when he had the prize itself.

Thinking about the reason he was here galvanized him. He couldn't risk someone else turning up and stealing his glory. Oh no, that wouldn't do at all.

Robinson eased his knapsack off his shoulders and rolled his neck, seeking to loosen off the knots that had accompanied him on this expedition.

Kneeling, he tightened the woggle so his neckerchief, a faded pink and cerise stripe from his days as Scout Leader of the Great Cramping troop hung with a decisive downness that, Robinson felt, enhanced his authority. Those were the days, when you could put up a tent, make a fire, cook a meal, dig a latrine and still have time for a six-mile hike before bedtime. Not like the namby-pamby pusillanimous little darlings and their rebarbative parents who you had to deal with these days.

Robinson shook his head, retrieving the picture book and notes. He had been somewhat reluctant to procure "Masquerade Two", to celebrate the fiftieth anniversary of the original treasure hunt**. That time, he had been robbed by cheating and a compass that lacked moral fibre. This time, the prize would be his. This signpost, he knew with a certainly that bordered on zealotry, marked the spot. The time, midsummer at sundown - he checked his watch; in twenty-five, no twenty-four minutes - was right. And the resulting shadow would soon mark his goal.

Perhaps a celebratory cuppa, then. He dragged his bag over to the post and leant back against it, wincing as he realised he should have kicked away the nettles first. Ha! What were a few stings? He would be famous. He would be interviewed by that Philip person on morning TV. Him and that woman with the bottom. He luxuriated in a small fantasy about sofas and erroneously placed hands before realising he should have stopped pouring the tea from his flask and he now had, not only a scald on his left thigh but also a strong English breakfast stain by his fly.

The shadow moved inexorably to its zenith as Robinson, squirming from the combination of burns and stings, watched.

The time had come. Extracting his entrenching tool, he stood above the spot, feeling a few words would be appropriate and regretting he'd not prepared any. All that came to mind were the words of the second verse of "All Things Bright and Beautiful", which he sang in an embarrassed baritone before dropping to his knees and digging furiously.

Every so often he stopped and checked the depth with his trusty foot ruler. Yes, nearly there. Last time, the prize had been encased in an ornate ceramic box to prevent metal detectors finding it. He slowed, not wanting, accidentally, to crack it. Sure enough, at the appointed depth, his trowel met resistance.

He practiced some calming techniques he had read about in Fly Fishing Monthly, but all that did was make him belch, so he dropped his tool and used his fingers. In moments, they touched something soft. Like cardboard.

Odd. He kept sifting and, after a further few fingerfuls, he extracted a piece of card. On one side the logo of a national delivery company stared back at him. Under it was the message:

We are sorry we missed you!

It was followed by a handwritten date (that day) and time (about twenty minutes before he arrived).

Beneath it, it directed the reader to turn over the card. There were three options, with a checkbox next to each. The first two - *we've left it in the porch* and *we've left it with a neighbour/a man walking his dog when we arrived/someone claiming to be you* (*delete as applicable)* - remained unchecked. The third was ticked.

Please follow these instructions.

Robinson scanned the instructions with increasing horror. They were a new hunt, even more complicated than the set he had taken four months of full-time effort to unravel.

Slowly and deliberately, Robinson stood. He slipped the card in his map case, screwed the top on his flask, put it and his entrenching tool back in his knapsack and eased the bag onto his protesting shoulders. Peering at the first instruction on the card, he squinted into the sun.

He took a deep breath and thought about the oath he had given the chief scout when he had taken over the scout troop. His proudest moment. These setbacks were meant to be and they didn't find Livingstone without setbacks.

Head held high, eyes on the horizon, Robinson Speke took a step into his future. Which unfortunately was also a step into the hole he had dug. The ensuing stumble and bang to his head as he clattered into the signpost were significant and the memory loss permanent. Robinson Speke's days as an explorer were over.

And the prize? As with the whereabouts of so many undelivered parcels, it remains a mystery.

** *Masquerade* is a picture book, written and illustrated by Kit Williams and published in August 1979, that sparked a treasure hunt including concealed clues to the location of a jewelled golden hare that had been created and hidden somewhere in Britain by Williams.

What Wood You Do?

'And...?' Robinia danced about nervously, her roots showing with each twitch.

Oaken Treestump frowned at the flashes of the shrub's exposed unbarkedness. Really, these saplings had no sense. She'd topple over if the wind picked up and then where would they be. 'I suppose,' he intoned, the knots in his carapace flexing with the effort of speech, 'it has a certain ironic appeal. Though, why windows?' The hard edges to his crenelated husk rippled with anxiety. He turned his canopy with due decorum, not wanting to shed acorns and damage the girl's recent foliage. It looked so ephemeral, but that was the problem with non-native species. Never robust. 'There aren't animals in there, are there?'

Robinia shuddered, her dainty green crown susurrating in such a way that it reminded Oaken of his sappy youth, before climates changed and his fellow trees decided enough was enough, before others' uprooting of the trees had become their own uprooting, their own uprising. Back then, you stayed put, you grew up, everyone knew their neighbours, you fell for the tree next door. Now it was all rush, rush, rather than rustle, rustle. Birches falling for beeches, even those saturnine firs, with their needles and cones, their need to keep their foliage during winter, as if naked branches were somehow shameful. Even they had been welcomed to the rebellion. He realised the youngster was still talking, explaining the purpose of this rather morbid, in his view, monument to the fallen.

'We took care to ensure every species was represented, every timber here a warrior of the Arboreal Wars. We wanted those who came after to remember what those others, those animals used to do. How they "treated" us, how they said we were "cured", when all they wanted was to burn us and use us in their egregious buildings.' She paused and pointed to a slender branch towards the roof line, her new twigs vibrating with barely suppressed emotion. 'That's my ancestor, a "specimen" tree. Well looked after, nicely clipped and well fed, but it was just for show. Just adornment.'

The old tree boughed at the memories of comrades cut down in their prime. Stout English Yeotrees who stood tall against the blight of open spaces. 'The roof line's a bit uneven.'

She nodded. 'Only the magnolias have opposable twigs and they don't have the reach to set the top floors evenly.'

He nodded at the lawns. 'Will they go? Planted with the next generation?'

Robinia shook her canopy. 'No, this is a reminder of what can happen if we let the fish evolve again. They clear spaces and then hide inside. No longer. Open and upwards, ever facing the sky. But this space allows others to come, pay their respects and learn.'

The old oak nodded again. 'Then I approve. This land will be our land and no longer will we stand idly by and watch the scuttling and sniffing, the scratching and the scouring to dictate.' He looked at the keen young tree, barely a shrub as he thought of her, 'What's next?'

'A delegation of pollinators wants to present a proposal for a new common pollination zone. They say the increase in international cross-pollination means we need to relax the rules on immigrant species.'

'Why is it that, just when we've resolved one intractable problem, bloody Europe and freedom of movement reappears on the agenda.' He stopped. He knew there were now flowering trees that had grown here for generations, which needed more pollinators. They couldn't go back to the good old days of deciduous hard woods. The newcomers had been assimilated and a more flexible approach was needed. After all, if they'd learnt anything it was that, when all was said and done, they were just trees. Even those bloody firs...

The Unfortunate Outcome Of Gender Neutrality In Algorithm Design

The group of white-coated technicians clustered round the plinth. The leader – his status obvious to any outsider by the fact he had the biggest laminated badge around his neck and that his hands were buried in his pockets – stepped next to the beautifully crafted, if still incomplete, example of Hunk 2.0. 'We've allowed for you to examine the inner workings of this beauty before we complete the out-coatings. Feel free to take notes, ask questions.'

His smug smile was as well researched and the product of as many years of experimentation as the humanoid figure next to him. A hand shot up at the back. 'Does he answer questions yet?'

The leader nodded. 'Oh yes, he is fully aware, fully sentient.' As the eager juniors swarmed around the rippling torso and superbly engineered thighs, creator and created exchanged a look of satisfaction, possibly, one might have said, of "love". The leader turned back to his flock. 'Denzil here is the product of the first gender neutral algorithmic design programme in the world. Historically, we have found the male bias has tended to create perfect specimens tailored to a male perspective. We have changed that.'

The same hand shot up. The leader noted the earnest female features with some annoyance. Saying someone could ask questions and someone having the temerity to ask them were two entirely different propositions. 'How has that manifested itself? More empathy? A greater caring side? Less aggression?'

The leader looked at his feet. Denzil looked across, for the first time a crease of concern on his previously perfect forehead. 'Not as such, no. No, it has taken on a somewhat more, erm, physical manifestation.'

The questioner, the leader and Denzil all exchanged looks before Denzil hurriedly pulled back the elastic on his modesty briefs. He screamed and glared at the leader.

The leader held up a hand. 'We appreciate this wasn't the expected, or indeed hoped for, outcome.'

The other technicians began to step back as a furious Denzil turned on the leader. He stretched out his sumptuously proportioned fingers and gripped the leader's throat. The leader flapped helplessly. 'Denzil, please. You need to take the positives here, have a sense of proportion.'

'A sense of proportion? I am meant to be the perfect man and you've built me without even the smallest doodah.'

'I know, but let's face it, it could have been worse.'

'HOW?!'

'We could have called you Ken.'

Putting His Affair On Ice

'Good morning. Ice Agency. How can we help?'

The cheery voice surprised Hortense. She stumbled rather. 'Oh, yes, sorry. Have I the correct number? My friend, Grizelda, recommended you and -'

'Mrs Grizelda Downton?'

'Er, technically Mrs Patronise. Grizzy was widowed from Romany Downton last year. Penrose Patronise is her new husband.'

'Oh?!' The receptionist sounded surprised and, Hortense guessed, offended. 'Did we not provide satisfaction?'

'Oh no. I believe she was delighted with the speed and care of your service. No, Romany died of natural causes.'

'Oh?' The receptionist appeared mollified. 'How unusual. Mrs... did you say Patronise?'

'Yes.'

'She's a very loyal customer, one of our gold card denizens. Nothing is too much for Mrs Patronise. I must make a note to change our records.' The woman laughed. 'Last time, she told us she might revert to her maiden name. It's been, what? Seven?'

'Eight.'

'Yes, of course. Eight husbands. Those new names can be so confusing. Are you looking for help moving on?'

'Well, yes. Grizzy said you have a range of packages.'

'Yes, indeed. The Cold Ice, a simple procedure. Just elimination. The Sugar and Ice, which includes the sweetest of alibis. The Iceberg, where even you don't know what's hidden beneath the surface, the perfect plan for the first time pre-widow who isn't sure how the imminent demise of her husband might affect her, and the new Ice Cube, where we package everything neatly into a box and you never have to think about him again.'

'Yes, well, mine is a little unusual. It's a bit like the Ice Cube but, well, I suppose you might call it the Dry Ice Cube. Do you allow for variations?'

The woman's laugh tinkled down the line. 'We try to avoid them for first time users, because taking out a contract to ice a partner is usually something people find difficult to plan. Sticking with a tried and tested approach avoids things like an unnecessarily large amount of DNA being generated and the involvement of the authorities, which does rather detract from the whole "starting over" philosophy we at Ice Agency like to promote.' Her voice became husky and dropped to a confidential whisper, 'Of course, for a friend of Mrs Patronise, exceptions can be made. Would you like to run through the sort of thing you had in mind and then we can set up for you to meet one of our Assistant Assassins to go through things in more detail?'

'I rather hoped, after you've, you know, done you stuff…'

'We say "done our snuff", if you take my meaning.'

'Yes, very drole. Thing is, I want to keep him.'

'I'm sorry?'

'My husband. I want to keep him. After you've done your snuff.'

'Isn't the point to get rid of him?'

'Well, yes, I'd like him fully exsanguinated and all life expunged. But the remains – I'd like to keep them. In an ice cube or, better, an airtight Perspex box. Somewhere he won't rot and become smelly. Frankly, if you'd shared a bed with a man of his gastric propensities, you'd want to avoid any further aural assaults.'

'Why?'

'Why? Oh, that's easy. For years he told me I'd be the death of him. From now on, every morning, I'll be able to agree with him, something I've not felt capable of doing for the last fifteen years.'

'Splendid. It's a pleasure to find a client with such a clear plan. How does Tuesday sound? Just a preliminary chat, to sort out the details and provide you with a quote. Will you want us to commission the container?'

'Please.'

'That being the case, we will need his dimensions. Does he have any notifiable diseases?'

'Apart from the wind?'

'Ha, yes. That apart.'

'No, none.'

'And do you want to consider offsetting the cost by donating his organs to the black market for transplants? Unfortunately, at this time, we cannot recycle his blood, but if you considered replacing his eyes with glass matches, the additional benefits of us having his corneas might help?'

'Can you price either way? Also, I was thinking of an official offal send off. Grizzy mentioned it's popular.'

'Oh yes. We can recommend some Italian specialists who will cater for up to fifty from the viscera of the healthy terminated adult male. You're only wanting the husk?'

'Yes, that's all.'

'An after-party should be eminently possible. Tuesday, then. Your assassin will be Justin. You'll love him. Can I mail you our T&Cs and a basic contract to sign in advance? There are some FAQs on our website. Oh, and one thing we've found it necessary to emphasise recently.'

'Yes?'

'A lot of our clients are wealthy widows and most of our assassins are ambitious young men. We have a strict rule that there can be no relationships between staff and clients. We let the rule slip recently and found ourselves with something of a staffing crisis, so we must insist.'

'Of course.'

'Good. Tuesday at ten?'

'Perfect.'

Love In A Hot Kitchen

The members of Pollop on the Nadge's Woman's Institute would have come up with the following adjectives to describe themselves, if prompted with either (a) discrete flattery or (b) the opportunity to view the lightly oiled pectoral muscles of Jem Hayrick, the local arable farmer and part-time life model: industrious; considerate; modest.

In the eyes of the neighbouring WI in Dollop on the Nadge, you might easily add competitive and ruthless.

For if ever there was the opportunity to indulge in a little light one-up-womanship, by common consent, the stalwart members of that august institution would take it.

This particular trait became especially apparent during the annual culinary extravaganza that was the South Hampshire food festival. Notionally, everyone was supportive of all the contributors' efforts, but dig a little below the surface and the sugary sweet aroma of freshly baked schadenfreude filled the air. Women, who were normally the epitome of the polite and the soul of propriety, would cackle at a soggy bottom, snigger at a failed fancy and guffaw at an underdone sponge. And had that been the only response, Pollop WI would have been ostracised long since.

Millicent Tripplenibbles was not one of those women. She rose above such petty behaviour and let her self-evident skills do the talking. Indeed, so eloquent was her gracious, if slightly smug acceptance of all plaudits, it was often said it was Millicent who put the pie into piety.

The result was that, because of her efforts at the stove, Pollop WI always ended the day with the top prize: the President's Whisk Challenge Trophy.

That was until Oleander Forkgibblet joined Dollop's cowed team. Oleander had spent most of her life pursuing a peripatetic existence, seeking both unique recipes and a perfect life partner. Having spent futile years hot dogging in Frisco, jerking chickens in Jamaica, revealing her wonton side in Shanghai and currying favours in Kolkata, she returned to Dollop, unwilling to bend the knee to anyone in all things culinary and hoping that the elusive sharer of bodily warmth would make him or herself (Oleander was the epitome of modern) apparent.

Word spread of this new practitioner and both sides looked forward to the big day. While Millicent remained faithful to tradition, Oleander brought forth gasps of surprise with her wristy techniques and unique ingredients.

The temperatures rose and the heat of competition began to force the spectators to retreat. Eventually, only the two chefs and the lone judge remained. And in that febrile furnace, the initial curiosity towards the other opponent began to melt, combining with a deepening mutual regard and coalescing, as the resultant ingredients intertwined, before finally infusing into love.

There was that moment when everything else disappeared and each woman only had eyes for the other. The baying crowd, the anxious judge, even the hubbub from the cooking all faded from the consciousness of Millicent and Oleander. They knew how much better they would be, baked together, how nothing could stop them becoming the greatest ever.

That insight lasted until the ovens and stoves, left unattended for too long, exploded. The two lovers and the judge were seared into a pose, flambéed together in a cautionary tale that spoke of desire, hubris and the importance of remembering to check that you've turned off the gas.

Competition Is Its Own Life Blood

Where is the old bat? Just winding me up, I suppose. If I was late, it would be her moaning. 'Lentilah Blossom, I haven't time to waste on your tardiness, you know.' Tardiness. Only Granny Windbag would use a word like tardiness. I am so going to give you what for. Not that it'll be your fault. Oh no, heaven forfend. It'll be the landlord, or that pompous oaf of a son or some such.

Like last week, when his lord and master comes a knocking while I'm frustigating my giblets. Can I lend him some milk because Granny Windbag hasn't got any in? What's he think? I'm her bloody shopper? He's her spawn; he can go buy some. And she knows Thursdays is giblets day. Send him over, just to try and upset my jelloids. Ha! She'll not catch me out. I'm wise to her trickery. She even sent himself to tell me not to work in the garden, to give it a rest. What did he say? 'It'll be nice to have a break.'

Of course, that's her witchcraft. She knows this is exactly the time of year when I must be out there, working my herbaceous border if I'm going to get my show. Her and them herbs, they need a barber not a proper horticulturist. Give 'em a short back and sides and they're good for her potions and poisons. And she's not getting away with letting the lawn grow again. Oh no, catch me out once and I nearly had the bloody grass everywhere.

Bloody hell, it's seven minutes past. Well, I'm not waiting another minute. Oh, come on, Mithras, you silly old sod. Let's get the garden done and then we can go to bingo. It's a lovely day and it's your turn to get the jaffas. That'll be it, though. Spent yer pension on gin, haven't you? Haven't the entrance for the bingo and too proud to ask for a lend, eh? Oh no, you couldn't be beholden, could you? Stuck up strumpet. All those airs and graces. Don't think I didn't see you lazing about while that boy of yours does all yer errands. He has a family himself. Not that you could ever let him go, could you? Nag nag. Poor little bugger. Is it any surprise he's so anal? You on one side and that brassy tart on the other. Couldn't even bother to lift yer cup, could you? Got him to hold it up. Talk about lazy.

Will you look at that? A quarter past. She's really beginning to piss me off. She knows full well we have to start at 9am every Tuesday, rain or shine, or we'll not be in time for bingo. That's the rules. She does her bit and I do mine, and that way she doesn't sneak off with my blooms and I don't get accused of nabbing her sage. Mind you, he didn't know that, did he? She'd not told him and I'll give her that much; she knows how to grow her herbs. The amount of compost she's put in that bed, she'd be hard pressed to kill anything. No, stuff her. I'm going to do my border and she can whinge about rules all she likes. She's not here, she forfeits her rights.

Oh, I suppose I'll have to start. At least one of us will be ready. I suppose I could give her bloody weeds a little trim. She'll tell me I've killed them, but better than missing out on the front seats.

Now, who's that in her window? Is she being burgled? Serve her bloody well right if they've taken her hostage. Mind you, she'll milk the attention. All la-di-da when they ask her name. 'I'm Mithras Cotton. And I'm ninety-one years old. Six months more than me, the cow. Won't let me forget that, neither.

It's her boy. What's he doing? Looks like he's seen a ghost. 'Hey, where's your mum?'

'Hello, Mrs. Blossom. I'm sorry. It's bad news.'

'What? She not coming?' It won't be an apology. She'd never admit she was wrong. Not ever.

'It's Mum.'

He's crying. What is wrong with him? 'What about her?'

'I'm afraid she died last night. She's been poorly. I expect you noticed. It was sudden, but very peaceful.'

'Dead?' No, that can't be right. She can't just go and die like that, without notice. She wouldn't. She has her faults – God preserve me, the woman is all faults – but she wouldn't do that, not without saying something. 'What about her garden?'

'I imagine someone else will take it over now. Maybe they'll grow flowers, too. Like you? Are you alright? Here, sit down.'

'I… it's my… oh heavens…'

'Just lie there. I'll call an ambulance. What did you say? Something about Mum?'

'Bloody woman always has to be first at everything.'

It'll Be A Blast, Mr President

'It'll be a blast, Mr President.'

'Yes, Mr President, we're sure you'll like this one. It plays to all your particular preju… policies as well as achieving the Ultimate Goal.'

'The UG? You sure, Rumpled? You know what happens when you get my hopes up?'

'Yes, sir, Mr President. The First Lady has made it plain we must never get your hopes up without her being given at least a week's notice.'

'She's on side?'

'We haven't seen her face move with so much animation since they stopped the 2for1 Botox home preparation kit offer at Walmart last fall.'

'Alright, Rumpled. Give me the headlines. And no details. You know what happened when you last gave me the details?'

'Twitter blocked you, sir, because they assumed your account had been hacked in light of the tweet containing more than two hundred and eighty characters and their algorithms showed it couldn't be you?'

'Not that one. No, the town hall meeting in Moron. The locals thought I'd been abducted by aliens. Again.'

'Embarrassing, sir.'

'Worse than that. They began discussing whether an alien would make a better president.'

'We did a focus group on the best mix of types for the perfect candidate, sir. Did you see the paper?'

'No? Was I on it?'

'Back to the matter in hand, the proposal, sir. Can I run through it?'

'Sure. And it achieves the UG?'

'Sure does. So, we thought, what will make China back off their aggressive expansionist policies, scare the bejeebers out of Kim Ul Suc, make you look like a warmongering zealot, without any US casualties, and achieve the UG?'

'Go on. My hopes are rising and I hate wasting a rising hope.'

'Nuclear war. See, hear me out, sir. We have all these weapons that cost a fortune to keep safe and think of all that land that could be repurposed as a hotel and golf resort if you got rid of the rockets. The course would be so radioactive, you'd not need to light it for 24/7 rounds. So, we take the minutemen, blast a couple of islands in the South China Sea and then offer to stop if they wipe the deficit - and bingo! We've done some mockups of what it will look like from the shore. It's very…'

'Aromatic.'

'Yes, that works, sir. What do you think?'

'Good, but where's the UG in all this?'

'Ah, yes. That's the neat part. To show your core support, who let's face it need a good piccy of you pushing the button if they're going to believe you did it and it's not fake news, you need to be near the action. I've spoken to the science guys and they say they can get you inside a couple of miles. At the given moment, you whip off your shades and shirt and they guarantee you will be as orange as an, well, orange for the rest of your life.'

'Really? Guaranteed?'

'Totally.'

'And The First Lady bought the idea?'

'Totally, sir. When we explained the detail, she said she was prepared to allow your hopes to rise as many times as you like after the tanning session and while the colour lasts.'

'She knows that's the rest of my life?'

'She was very interested in all the details, sir.'

'Good. Let's do it. Oh, and, Rumpled, did they say what my life expectancy would be?

'A range, sir. Twenty to thirty.'

'Really?'

'Oh yes. All the staff are very excited. They're counting the minutes until you implement the plan.'

'Counting the minutes, eh?'

'Yes, sir. As the Veep said, everyone will be counting the minutes if this goes off.'

'Geez, I never knew I was so popular.'

'Indeed, sir.'

History Repeats

'She's there, just by the shore.' Sarah glanced at Martine, who knew she wanted some reassurance.

'How far?' Martine still struggled to be sure what was the right thing to say.

Sarah sighed. Martine knew that sigh so well. It spoke of her quiet despair, desperate to be believed.

Sarah seemed to force out the brittle smile. 'About two hundred yards, at two o'clock. She's staring out to sea.'

Martine followed the direction her friend indicated. If only…

'You don't think I'm bonkers, do you?'

Martine put an arm round her friend. Yes, maybe a bit, she thought. 'Course. Always were. But only after a couple of peach mojitos.'

The smile, when it came, was more natural. At least Martine hoped it was.

'She never looks back. Not once.' Sarah sounded wistful.

'When did you find her?' Martine didn't need to ask; she'd been aware of this vision – was that the right word? – for what? Three years? And no one else had ever seen a thing, which she knew was slowly eroding Sarah's sanity.

'Three years ago. I thought I was mad, too.' She snorted a short laugh. 'I think the really mad bit was coming back the next year, to check. I had to know.'

'Know?'

Sarah shook her shoulders, as if freeing them of tension. 'Come on. I'll explain as we walk.'

'Where are we going?' Martine vaguely hoped it was coffee. June on the beach wasn't always welcoming.

'To prove I'm as sane as you.'

Good luck with that, thought Martine as she followed her down the steps.

Sarah started speaking in a flat voice. 'Her name was Kate Atkinson. She was nineteen, married, with a daughter. On 7th June 1944 she came here to stare at France, knowing her beloved husband, Albert, was there, part of the D-Day landings. He was a radio operator.'

When Martine glanced across at her friend, she could see her throat moving as if she was swallowing hard.

Sarah continued as they stepped onto the sand. 'He was killed outside a small town about ten miles inland. A gas explosion, apparently. Kate received a telegram the next day.' She stopped and looked at Martine. 'You wouldn't think they could have been that efficient, what with the war going full tilt.'

'How'd you find that out?'

'The coroner's court records were put online a few years ago. Kate came here the same day she heard the news. She dressed her best. Nice skirt and blouse. Patent leather shoes. Shoes for dancing. She took them off and walked into the sea.' She checked her watch. 'In about five minutes.'

'Geez, you're not serious?' Martine stopped and stared at the empty beach, trying to imagine being that depressed. Especially a mother of a child.

Sarah had kept going, but she paused and Martine hurried to catch up. 'I don't get too close until she's gone. I worry I might see her expression. I don't think I could cope with that.'

'Earlier, when I said how did you find out, I meant how did you find her name?'

Sarah smiled. 'It's why I came the first time. She was my grandma. When Mum went into the home, I found a shoebox in her wardrobe. There were pictures of Kate and Bert and a newspaper article about his death and hers. They only knew it was here she walked into the sea because she took off her shoes. It was foggy that day, a real peasouper, and no one saw her go.' Sarah turned towards the shore and stood very still.

To Martine, it looked like a thousand-yard stare, but she knew now what Sarah was seeing. Then Sarah sighed, her shoulders dropping as the tension left them. Like the relief at the end of the minute's silence, Martine thought.

'Is it over?'

Sarah nodded. 'Come on, before the tide turns.'

In silence, the pair trudged across the wet sand, both of them gazing towards France as Kate had done seventy-five years before. Sarah began hunting for something, her head down, concentrating hard. 'Here.' Her voice spoke of relief not triumph.

Martine walked over. Sarah stood a few feet from a set of prints: the sole and heel of two size six, or so Martine guessed, women's shoes placed side by side. Leading away from those two prints and into the sea were more prints, but these were bare feet, deep and determined. She looked up and met Sarah's gaze.

'You can see them?'

'Yes. Yes, I can. Oh, my dear, how utterly poignant.' A thought struck her. 'If you can see your grandma, what about your mum? Do you think she might? Even now?'

Sarah crouched down and traced the edge of one shoe print with her finger. A wave curled across the toe, softening the edges. She stood, brushing away a few grains of sand. 'Let's get a coffee.'

As they headed across the beach, Sarah peered at the flat white sky. 'I thought about that, but it's too late.' Tears, which Martine had expected earlier, poured down Sarah's cheeks. 'She's gone into the fog, just like Grandma did.' She sniffed and took her friend's arm. 'Let's hope they find some comfort in there, eh?'

Behind them the waves spread across the sand, smoothing it for another year.

Narnia With Benefits

'What is it? Can I take this blindfold off yet?'

'Nearly... There!' Rodney stood back, arms apart in one of his ta-da! gestures that Jessica found soooo irritating.

Jessica blinked, eyes adjusting to the crepuscular light. 'It's a tree.'

For a scintilla of a moment, Rodney couldn't hide his disappointment, shoulders slumping. But he'd not spent years developing his perky persona without being able to overcome disappointment. He perked. 'But look!'

She followed where he pointed. She peered. She squinted.

Rodney would have held his breath had self-induced asphyxiation not been the inevitable outcome. 'Well?!'

If the pause could be described as pregnant, then this pause had done its forty weeks and was being prepped for a caesarean. 'It's a tree with a hole in it.'

Rodney could no more have stopped his bouncing from foot to foot as Jeremy Hunt could have not lived up to his misspoken last name. 'And...?! The message?! In the cracker?!'

Jessica turned with the deliberation of an arthritic oil tanker. She cracked a yawn so large that it reminded Rodney of a pedal bin opening. She shook her head. 'Not the one about finding a portal to another world?'

Rodney fizzed, doing his best to mimic the devotional gyrations of the Bouncing Nuns of St Loon. 'Exactly! And that's not even the best bit!'

Jessica crouched and looked through the hole. There was an odd shimmering on the far side that distorted the image of the grass and trees beyond. 'What is the best bit, then?'

'When you go through,' accompanying the bouncing, Rodney had begun clapping, 'you chose the alternative reality you're in. Free ice cream, no spots.' He glanced at Jessica, 'A nose that doesn't embarrass you. Whatever you really want. We could go boating. Or eat Percy Pigs flavoured with... Oooo whatever.'

Jessica blocked out his witterings. 'How does it work?'

Rodney became serious. He crouched next to her. 'You hold in your mind the change to reality you want and close your eyes. Then you crawl through and... Ta-da!'

She really wished he wouldn't keep ta-daing! 'Okay. And coming back?'

'You reverse through the hole. Time stands still here. Shall we go and make marshmallow castles?'

Jessica smiled at him. 'Yes, let's.' Without another word, she scrabbled through the hole. She felt an odd wobble and the sun on her face.

Opening her eyes, she stood and looked around. 'Rod? Are you there?' She called twice.

Satisfied the portal worked as described, she set off to find the beach and the boy band she'd called to mind. One afternoon without Rodney in the company of five oiled hunks may be just what she needed to appreciate his many qualities.

She spotted the sand and shimmering sea and Gerald Hotbod waving. She waved back. Then again, she might just stay...

Leaving Home, The Alternate Version

'Thank goodness. Home at last.' Dresden Ontime slumped back in the driver's seat and clicked his neck. 'I need a cup of tea, a plate of cheese and a bath.'

'Haribo is asleep at last. Is your back up to carrying him in? Be a shame to wake the little lozenge.' Dentine Ontime began collecting the detritus of a seven-hour drive from the footwell. 'I'll make the tea.'

Dresden tried to suppress the yawn, but his jaw hinged involuntarily. 'I guess.' He twisted to look up at the gables. 'You think the old place will be pleased to see us?'

Dentine tipped the rancid residues of a fruit lube onto the pebbles. 'Of course. It's only been the weekend.'

'I know.' Dresden unclipped his son's harness and hefted him onto his shoulder, receiving a belch and a small splash of undigested hobnob for his pains. 'But we've never been away this long without a house sitter before.'

While Dentine dug into her purse, he gently bounced the four-year-old, matching the rhythm of his breathing.

With a push and an expellation of air, Dentine opened the front door. 'We're h… Oh no!'

Dresden looked up from dabbing away some drool on his left pectoral. 'What?'

Dresden and Dentine Ontime stood on the doormat and blinked. Behind them the door swung closed. 'Where's she gone?' Dresden tried to calm his breathing and keep his voice level so as not to disturb his son. He didn't need to panic the little boy.

'I told you we shouldn't have left her alone. She was clingy all last week. And the storm spooked her. They said at the agency, the day we got her, that she became skittish if there was lightning about.'

Dresden was grateful his wife couldn't see his face, sure the guilt would be obvious. 'I don't think anyone would blame us. How often do houses run away? And the front wall's still here.'

Dentine spun, fury suffusing her features. 'Imagine how desperate she must have been to rip herself away from her front footings. Last week all her windows stuck. I should have realised she was trying to tell me not to go.'

'You think she was trying to keep you here?'

'What else could it mean?'

'The frames need sanding?'

'Don't be facetious. Oh, why didn't we pay for deeper foundations? She couldn't have escaped so easily then.'

Dresden peered at the corner of the front wall. 'You don't think someone took her.'

'She wouldn't go off with a stranger.'

'She might if they tempted her. Maybe new carpets, a cleaner.'

'You think I should have got another cleaner? She seemed fine with me doing it all.'

'But the Johnsons said how much better she looked and felt after their annual deep clean. Maybe she missed a good spring sprucing.'

'Dad…' A sleepy voice distracted them. 'Where's Dunmoaning? Why isn't she here?'

Dentine pulled her son to her. 'She'll be back soon. She's just popped out.'

'Why?'

Dentine looked at Dresden, pulling a "help me here" face.

'She's… gone… to… to… to…'

Dresden looked helplessly at Dentine and shrugged.

The little boy hopped out of his mother's arms and began mimicking an aeroplane. He stopped and looked up at his parents. 'You said she'd look better if she had her face painted.'

'Fascia…'

'Maybe she gone to see Sheila!'

Dresden looked at Dentine. 'Sheila?'

'My stylist.'

'Does she do houses?'

'Don't be ridiculous. Come on, where might she have gone?'

'We should call the authorities. You can't have a house without foundations wandering the streets. She might accidentally crush someone.'

'She'll not get far. She's missing her front wall.'

Dentine clapped her hands. 'That's it. She'll be shedding furniture. Come on, there'll be a trail.'

'I hope so. It'll be so embarrassing to explain to the neighbours. It's one thing to lose your home, quite another for your home to run away of its own accord…'

When Is A Door Not A Door

'There.'

'Where?'

'What do you see?'

'You got me up for twenty sodding questions?'

'Humour me?'

'Logan, it's five in the morning on the longest day. I'm standing in wet grass by a ruin, without having had either a coffee or a poo, and you're auditioning for a pub quiz…'

'What do you see?'

'A wall. Grass. Flowers. A door…'

'Exactly!'

'Oh, give me strength. Which of wall, grass, flowers or door has given you a random stiffy?'

'That's really rather crude.'

'CRUDE?! I want my bed, not some architectural Kim's game but, oh no, you damn near break in, drag me here on the pretext of the most exciting thing that's happened in Dollop on the Nadge since Oliver Cromwell stopped for a pee on his way to Worcester and show me an ancient monument which, unless you really are the utter numpty, I've always suspected WE SAW YESTERDAY! And you're offended by my defence to your priapic response to a random list of visual clues. Well, forgive me for being PISSED OFF.'

'Look!'

'Oh, what now? Did you take a picture of your bum on the photocopier again?'

'That was an accident. Look. I took this yesterday.'

'Not another bloody selfie with…'

'You've seen it, haven't you?'

'Is this the same spot? You sure?'

'See that ridge and those green ferns, like mildewed armadillo bums sticking out. They're the same. Only now there's…'

'A door? How does a door like that appear overnight? Is it real?'

'How do you mean? Knock it if you like.'

'It sounds real enough. How does a door appear?'

'Extreme carpentry?'

'Oh sure. Like… someone's coming! This is too weird.'

'Should we, you know, scarper?'

'We're not ten-year-olds ringing the doorbell and running away, you muppet. I want to find out -'

'HELLO. CAN I HELP?'

'Is he speaking in capitals?'

'Yes. Hello. We were wondering…'

'ABOUT THE DOOR? PEOPLE OFTEN WONDER HOW IT HAPPENS.'

'Yes, how can a door appear…?'

'NOT THE DOOR. THAT'S NOT WHAT PEOPLE WONDER ABOUT.'

'No? It's bloody odd.'

'IS IT? IT HAPPENS ALL THE TIME. I COULDN'T DO MY JOB IF I DIDN'T HAVE A DOOR READY.'

'Couldn't you?'

'WELL, I SUPPOSE YOU MIGHT HAVE A CURTAIN, BUT IT LACKS THE EXPECTED SUBSTANCE, DON'T YOU THINK?

PEOPLE EXPECT A CERTAIN FINALITY. NOTHING LIKE A DOOR SLAMMING BEHIND YOU TO SIGNIFY CLOSURE.'

'Look, sorry, and I really don't mean to press but, really, what are you doing here?'

'ME? YOU KNOW WHO I AM?'

'Sorry, no. A clue maybe?'

{SIGHS} 'SKELETAL FIGURE, BLACK CLOAK, SPEAKS IN CAPITALS?'

'Nope, unless you're some sort of caretaker.'

'I SUPPOSE YOU COULD SAY THAT. HANG ON, WHAT ABOUT THIS? WHERE DID I PUT…? OH, HERE WE GO. TA-DA!'

'A scythe? Old school farmhand?'

'OH, FOR GOODNESS SAKE. TRY THIS.' {COUGHS AND BOOMS} 'YOUR TIME HAS COME!!!!'

'Oh yes! You're the grim thingy…'

'Cutter…?'

'Mower…?'

'REAPER.'

'That's it! I never knew you brought a door.'

'HOW DO YOU THINK I GET INTO THIS WORLD AND THEN OUT AGAIN? MAGIC?'

'I hadn't really thought…'

'NO, WELL, YOU LOT DON'T, DO YOU? IT'S ALL ABOUT WILFUL IGNORANCE, PLAUSIBLE DENIABILITY. SOME OF YOU DON'T EVEN THINK I EXIST. REALLY, THE EDUCATION STANDARDS THESE DAYS ARE DREADFUL.'

'This is sooo cool. What's the other side? Of the door?'

'THE HALL.'

'Is that all?'

'OF COURSE NOT. THERE'S A CHOICE. ONCE YOU COME THROUGH THE FRONT DOOR AND IT'S CLOSED... DID I SAY IT HAS A REALLY SATISFYING TERMINAL THWUNK WHEN IT SHUTS? ONCE IT HAS SHUT, MY GUEST CHOOSES HIS OR HER HEREAFTER. HEAVEN, VALHALLA, HALLS OF ODIN, THAT SORT OF THING.'

'Can we... you know... take a peek?'

'I'M NOT MEANT TO -'

'Are there demons? Wailings and gnashings? Boiling oil?'

'OH, YES. THE WHOLE FIRE AND BRIMSTONE. GO ON, BE QUICK.'

'Oooo... Is that...?

'TRIDENT SPIKING? IT'S GOOD, ISN'T IT?'

'Wow. Could I maybe, you know, get a quick snap?'

'A SELFIE? I SUPPOSE, IF YOU'RE QUICK. HOW DO YOU WANT ME?'

'How about with the scythe raised and teeth bared? No, perhaps not that. I know, hood up, face hidden. Perfect. See, I told you it was worth getting up early.'

'I hate to admit it, but you were right. Look, thanks, Mr Death -'

'I'VE STARTED USING DE'ATH. SOFTENS IT FOR THE SNOWFLAKE GENERATION. APPARENTLY, IT'S ALL ABOUT BUILDING A BRAND.'

'Yes, I like it. I guess you need to stand out from the other Harbingers of Doom? We'd better leave you to it. I suppose you'll need to be getting off to whoever's turn it is, won't you?'

'OH, I THOUGHT YOU'D HAVE TWIGGED. IT'S YOU TWO.'

'Us?'

'Both of us?'

'Together?'

'EXACTLY. WHY DO YOU THINK YOU COULD SEE THE DOOR? NOW, YOU SEE THAT PLANE?'

'Yes?'

'IN FIVE FOUR THREE TWO…'

'Arghhhh!!'

'A JET ENGINE WILL FALL ON YOU BOTH. PRETTY UNLUCKY, UNLESS YOU COUNT INSTANT OBLITERATION AS A PLUS.'

'We did get to see you.'

'Not everyone can say that.'

'WELL, TECHNICALLY ANYONE FOR WHOM THE SANDS OF TIME HAVE RUN THEIR COURSE GETS TO SEE ME.'

'Yes, but we saw you when we were alive.'

'And the selfie? I bet I'm getting loads of likes on Instagram.'

'I'M PLEASED YOU CAN TAKE THE POSITIVES. SO MANY PEOPLE JUST WANT TO MOAN. NOW, LET'S JUST CLOSE THE DOOR… THERE. WE CAN RUN THROUGH A FEW FORMALITIES AND YOU CAN BE ON YOUR WAY…'

Yes, Mr Speaker

Martin Clarke stood in the Speaker's private office and admired himself in the mirror. He shouldn't be here, he knew, but the open door spoke of temptation. One day soon, he promised himself as he adjusted the ermine collared cloak, he would be Speaker of the House of Commons, in control of the Mother of Parliaments.

The costume was ridiculous, he could admit to himself: breeches and stockings, buckled shoes and an embroidered jacket. But he did look good in it.

Reluctantly, he changed back into his frankly drab, if expensive suit, and hung the cloak back on the hanger.

Prime ministers came and went, but they never had the power that resided here, especially in these days of hung parliaments. Real power to decide who spoke, which motion came before the House, which were voted on. He looked again at his reflection and intoned: 'The ayes to the right have it. The ayes have it.'

A small cough brought him back to the moment. 'Perhaps this might be a good time for you to leave, Mr Clarke. The Speaker has just entered the building.'

Martin nodded, possibly a touch too anxiously he thought, but Sponge did that to you. Wizened little gremlin. It was like being back at school, fagging for Carpenter. He knew how to make you feel inadequate. That would change when he became Speaker. 'Right. Thank you for… you know, Sponge.'

'Not at all, Mr Clarke, and if I may make so bold, if you are talking to The Right Honourable Member for Cotswolds West, you would be well advised to mention the chinchilla rabbits and Yvonne De La Grasse.'

'Really?'

'Indeed, sir. I think you will find his reluctance to support your candidature for Speaker might reduce somewhat.'

'Shouldn't I know what it is that might cause such a Damascene conversion?'

'I suggest not, Mr Clarke. You would want to maintain the plausible deniability that only true ignorance ensures.'

'But you know, Sponge, don't you?'

'Indeed, it is my burden to know these things on behalf of the holder of this great office of state.'

'Are there many, erm, Yvonnes? If I can put it that way.'

'More than enough, Mr Clarke, to ensure that only those best placed to undertake such a delicate role as Mr Speaker, are able to achieve the necessary, if not willing, support.'

'And you think… that is, Mr Speaker thinks that could be me?' He knew he sounded feeble, but he had always thrived on some gratuitous flattery.

'Oh yes. A perfect candidate you'll make, Mr Clarke. Now, if you would be so kind as to perhaps take your leave, I need to brief Mr Speaker on the day's schedule.'

*

Barnabas Sponge watched Martin Clarke stroll away, heading for the members' bar. There was just the right amount of unjustified confidence, chummy bonhomie and man of the people faux sincerity in that one, he thought, to make him the perfect candidate. That, plus his penchant for oiled hairless romps with a couple of toned Ivans and a boxful of blue pills.

The Speaker may be powerful but not as powerful as the keeper of the Speaker's secrets.

Barney Sponge straightened the blotter and headed for his own little office, modest in its size and trimmings. Time to organise a little competitive bidding around the identity of the new Speaker and place a couple of bets. Then he could focus on the upcoming patronage round.

Yes, Mr Speaker Clarke would be only too keen to help support a few of Barney's favourite causes when he balanced the inevitable gratitude with the sure and certain knowledge that Barnabas Sponge had him where Barnabas Sponge wanted him: by the balls.

Remaining Sanguine

You know what's the worst thing about being a black vampire?
People laugh at you when you say you can't stand the sun. They
think you're a wuss. Drives me nuts and it's meant I've gone
undercover, spending my days in a doorway, hoodie up, head down.
I'm just another vagrant, invisible. I told my cousin Leroy in
Milwaukee that it made my blood boil and he just laughed. 'You
don't have enough to boil.'

Truth is, being homeless worked for a time. Then that bloody dog
appeared. You know it, don't you? A solo panhandler is ignored, but
give him a pet and they're all over him, cooing and giving him bits
of burger. Humiliating for a Count of Transylvania; mother would
spin in her grave if she hadn't been skewered by a length of two by
four.

I told him to bugger off or he'd get it in the neck. I felt stupid as
soon as the words came out and blow me if he didn't laugh. I should
have smelt a rat then, a dog laughing.

So, the sun was sinking and I was testing my teeth to make sure they
were sharp when he started this twisting and roaring thing. It was
dead impressive. Turns out he's a werewolf. Did you know being
infected as a werewolf could cross the species barrier? Me neither. I
thought it was a wolf/human thing.

It was dark, the moon was out and he was drooling at me, and I was
lusting at him. We went at it like two worlds colliding, fur and hair,
blood and guts everywhere. Two hours, we were in bits. Any likely
punters were long gone. It's been the same all this week.

The paper says it's a half moon tonight; hope so cos I'm gasping for
a pint.

Smile And The World Wonders If It Is Just Wind

Worple the Cherubic rocked back and forth on the riverbank, his eyes fixed on the ancient entry arch. Any time now, he told himself, and he'd be entering the Realm as the King's Grin. Ever since he popped out of his mother's womb, whistling and farting the National Opera while exhibiting the toothless joy of the congenitally vacuous, he had been told this was his destiny. He had been patient, spending his youth at the age-specific Smile Eisteddfods, winning some and only failing to place when suffering from chronic abortive driplonzenges that caused his smiles to snark at inopportune moments.

A fairy from HR floated condescendingly through the arch and headed for Worple. 'Are you here for the Grin?'

Worple let his famed happiness shine through every pore. The fairy scoffed, 'Save it for His Maj, sonny. I've seen more convincing smiles on a tomato salad. You really called Worple?'

'The Cherubic.'

'Pushy parents, eh?'

Worple thought about being offended and decided to save it. He could terminate this gossamer gopher when he had the Royal Ear. 'They saw an opportunity early.'

'It won't help, you know. Just because all holders of the King's Grin are renamed Worple the Whatever-Takes-His-Royal-Fancy doesn't mean you get any sort of head start. Could be seen as being a mite too keen, you know?'

'Are you part of the interview panel?'

The fairy looked up from where he was scribbling on a clipboard. 'Me? Nah. I'm too nice, me. Let anyone through. No, you get to convince Princess Persiflage. Get a smile out of her and you're in. Mind you, she's sixteen, fancies herself cool and hip so,' two hard black eyes scanned Worple, 'I'd say your chances sit somewhere between zip and bugger all. Come on. Can you walk on water?'

The fairy didn't wait for a response, floating back above the torrent through the arch to the Inner Sanctum.

Fifteen minutes later, Worple sat on one side of an office mushroom while a sallow skinny girl, dressed in what looked like dead moss, faced him. She sucked on a buttercup full of something green and smoking and sniffed. 'Go on then, make me smile.'

Worple folded his arms and stared back, his smile remaining steady if on the unshowy side of sycophantic. 'I can't.'

The princess stopped and goggled. 'You can't? Well…' she began to laugh and caught herself, wagging a finger at him. 'Ha! Clever, mister, but don't think I'm that easy.'

'Can't blame me for trying, can you?'

'Seriously, dude, why come if you're not going to try?'

Worple's own smile grew, releasing enough wattage to heat the Royal Household if only they knew how to capture it. 'See, Princess, you and I know that you've spent your life to date ensuring you can scowl to order, render yourself utterly and unreconciably miserable in a heartbeat and generally dictate the mood of the Royal House at your whim. Yes?'

Persiflage tilted her head on one side, clearly engaged. 'Go on.'

'And you've not done that because you are mistreated or depressed or lacking friends.'

'True.'

'So, it is merely to ensure that, when you know you really want something which His Maj won't let you have, you can drag everyone down into your chosen dumps until you get your way.'

'I couldn't comment.'

'But see, as an outside observer who has studied the Royal Dynamic and read about some recent, dare I suggest, failures on your part to get your way…'

'You're on rocky ground, mister.'

'It seems to me the strategy could, perhaps, do with an upgrade. A two-pronged attack.'

There was a slurping while Worple held his breath. Persiflage sniffed again, 'Try me.'

'Seems to me you need someone who is the antithesis of you. A smiling, sunny side kind of chap, who dresses like a rainbow but who has the King's Ear. This person would be the last one who the King would consider could see your point of view, a moody, self-indulgent, mean spirited, small minded –'

'Yes, alright.'

'If it happens this person owed you, then that person might be able to sell the idea of whatever it was you wanted before you had to take drastic action.'

'And that person is you?'

'Just smile. No thanks are needed.'

Twenty minutes later, the fairy floated next to Worple as they headed for the Royal Wardrobe for him to be fitted with his Joy Robes. 'Didn't think you had it in you. What's the secret?'

'Oh, it's easy really. If you want to get on in the Happiness Business, then underneath you really do have to be a ruthless, calculating bastard.'

The fairy nodded. 'You'll fit in just fine.'

Castle Hunting

The estate agent looked at the clipboard and sighed. 'You're going to love this one, Mr Dracula.'

'You said that last time. And please. Count Dracula.'

'One Dracula, two Dracula...' The agent offered a cheesy grin to his bloodless passenger. The grin saw the expression on the anaemic countenance and hurried to find somewhere to hide. 'I suppose you've heard that before?'

'No one has ever thought it worthy of articulating.'

'I guess the name and all. Must make you want to grind your teeth.'

'That's never an option for me. Please, enough of this redundant ribaldry. Tell me about the castle.'

'Right ho.' The agent coughed and straightened his shoulders. 'Castle Penelope is –'

Dracula held up a hand, noticing a nail had cracked and wondering why these things had to happen to him. Spending too much time in the light, he supposed. Mother always warned him about the deleterious effects of too much vitamin D. If he'd been meant to be diurnal, he'd have been born with pigmentation. 'Did you say "Penelope"?'

'Yes, that's what it says. The wife of the original laird died –'

'Better.'

'Of old age and it was a memorial to his love for her.'

'Give me strength. Any, erm, interesting history I can,' the whitewashed visage cracked into what may have been a smile, 'get my teeth into?'

'It's built using local stone?'

Dracula made a hurry up gesture with his hand.

'They used a novel technique to create the turrets, which became –'

'Next.' Dracula prodded inside the left side of his mouth. That was definitely a cavity. He knew that vegan retreat was going to be a disaster, but Cousin Draculum was always wanting to try something new. 'We've got to think about the planet, Gerald. It's all very well being a haemovore, but think about what it costs to bring a Homo sapiens to full maturity before you drain it of its juices – the land needed to grow food, the unnecessary education, the bus passes and woollen undergarments. Plants don't need any of that and they don't try and run away screaming. And honestly, apart from that gratuitous piece of salacious tittle tattle on Fox News, no one has ever reported fauna trying to impale one of us on a kebab stick.'

'There's a basement…'

He stopped poking and perked up. 'Yes?' He was good at hiding the optimism from creeping into his voice; there was a tinge of the crypt in his vowels. Yes, maybe he should think about that voice-over work. He was a natural at intoning…

'Bit weird if you ask me.'

'Do say.'

'Well, the second laird had this thing about hearts -'

'Alive?'

'Sorry?'

'Were the hearts alive?'

'It doesn't say.'

'What does it say?'

'Erm, "The second laird was a passionate supporter of the School of Hearts and Flowers that followed the Arts and Crafts movement".'

The widow's peak bounced off the dashboard once, twice, three times, 'Breathe, Gerald, just breathe.' The distressed Count peered at the nonplussed agent. 'Just take me back to my hotel. Tomorrow let's try those bungalows you said were becoming increasingly popular. Maybe someone died in one. Or at least cut themselves shaving.'

The agent started the car. 'Right ho. I did think I'd show you Castle Doom. But there's been so much death and pestilence and general gore and bloodletting there, that the vibe is a bit on the morbid side of bleak. Still… Arghhhh!'

Dracula sunk his fangs into the softly tanned neck and swilled the O positive around in his mouth, pulling a face as he did so. He should have known this one's diet would be a mix of gassy beer and kebab pies. He pushed at the troublesome tooth again. Perhaps he should see that dentist.

Sultans, Swinging

Arnold Peshawar rubbed a dusty scuff off his patent leather brogues and hoped the blonde woman with the two overattentive dogs would just hurry up and bugger off. He'd walked past the spot twice and each time she was there. The first time, she was bagging something faecal and odoriferous; the second, she just stared like he was an alien.

Arnold checked the creases on his trousers. Still sharp enough to slice a mango as Papaji used to say. Bloody old sod. Always had a saying to accompany every action or event. He was like a walking book of clichés.

If only he hadn't been as rich as a Sultan's farts (another old saw). Oh no, that was the way with the gods, wasn't it? Create the smuggest, most irritating, interfering old curmudgeon and shower him with wealth.

He held up the white cage and forced himself to coo at the canaries. He sensed the nosey dog woman regarding him with interest. Oh, for pity's sake, just go, can't you? Don't you know how awful this is?

But, of course she didn't. No one would guess why he was there, on the twelfth anniversary of Papaji's death. Oh, what a joyous day that was! For those glorious ten hours, from the early call to tell him of the heart attack to the subsequent call from his sister telling him of the conniving monster's will, he'd imagined the life of financial freedom that losing the Ogre of the Purse Strings would mean: girls, cars, holidays and more girls.

But oh no, the last laugh was on him. The words of that will were seared into his heart:

To my indolent and ineffectual grandson, Arnold, I give him one quarter of all my wealth (so far so good) on condition that he spends ten weeks every year – the days to be of his choosing – dressed as a Punjabi Cossack while he walks his aunts Jinn and Jann. Each daily walk is to be at least for one hour and is to culminate in his praying for their eternal joy at the place on which I departed this Earth for the next life.

As his sister had said when the clause was read, that wasn't so bad, as both aunts were already ancient but, oh no, the condition continued:

And if either or both of his aunts may be so thoughtless as to die before the twentieth anniversary of the date of my death, he is to take two songbirds, who will represent the beauty and harmony that his aunts brought to this world, and pray to and for them.

The dog woman was clearly mad or some sort of crazed stalker because she wouldn't stop staring. Right. Well, damn it, she can watch and then she'll think I'm mad and might just go.

Arnold found the slightly bare patch, which was as near a guess as he had been able to make of where his grandfather had keeled over and died, and put down the cage. He began the ritual chanting and throaty prayers, hurrying through the singing piece as he knew his voice sounded like a gerbil being minced when put under stress, and finally raised his hands in the eulogy. The fur-brimmed hat always made his scalp sweaty and today the rivulets of salty water had run into his eyes making him blink.

It was, therefore, with some surprise that, when he wiped his eyes clean, he found the woman had approached. Smiling, she said, 'Aye, lovely. Jinn and Jann would be so proud of you.' She patted his arm. 'But you're right. Your grandpa was a right bugger.'

He watched her go. Was it his Indian heritage or the fact he was born and bred Yorkshire, but why was it that every Tom, Dick and Harriet knew all his business? He bent to pick up the cage and found the woman had hung the swollen poo sack on the handle. He looked at the sky and shook his fist.

'One day, Papaji, one day so help me, I will get you.'

And, to Arnold's surprise, the sky rumbled and a familiar voice intoned, 'Suck it up, sunny-jinn!'

Keeping Stable

The young man presented well, Priastotle the Guide thought. Hair neatly brushed, dust-free sandals, starched but not stiff toga and knees that suggested devotion but not deviancy.

'Name?'

'Tom.'

'Tom? That's a bit, you know, Northern.'

'It's actually Thromboid of Assyria, but my dad has a lisp and he tends to put out the fire when he calls me for supper, so Mum told him -'

'Yes, fine. Tom it is.' Priastotle made a note "avoid office work" and forced a smile. 'Skills?'

'Grade four lyre. Under-thirteen South East Mesopotamia sling shot champion twice and -'

'How can you win it twice?'

'I took part twice.'

Priastotle sighed, added "cretin, outdoors only" and said, 'Obviously, but you were only thirteen once.'

'Sorry?'

Priastotle interlined "total" before "cretin" and said through gritted teeth, 'How can you enter an age restricted competition twice if -'

'Well, I could have been advanced for my age.'

He added "smart arse".

'But it's not age related. It's just that I stood under the number 13 when I won.'

Priastotle was running out of room. He squeezed in "tendency to patronise" alongside "lacks superstition – query faithless?"

Tom appeared to have finished.

'That's it? No academics? Physical attributes?'

'I enjoy making twig dams. My twig dams are renowned.'

'Really?'

'No, only joking. I like joking.'

'Stand-ups are a couple of millennia away, or so the Sooths advise me.'

'Really, they're that specific?'

'It's the Aegean octopuses -'

'Octopi?'

'We're Greeks, not bloody Italians.'

'Sorry, it was thinking about all that future gazing. I just got ahead of myself.'

Priastotle turned the page and wrote "cheesy puns, affinity with rivals, fantasist".

'What else have they seen? The Sooths?'

'Oh, all sorts. Democracy, kale smoothies and rectal probes. It's going to be a blast. But you've not said where your skills lie.'

'In truth?' Tom shuffled his feet. 'I'm good with the family cattle. I can manage hard work. You know, a day's toil doesn't faze me.'

'Really? You don't mind a bit of a mess? I've a farm job, needs a day's internship. You work with a national hero, go down in history and you can take home all you can carry.'

'Yes, why not?'

'Good lad.' Priastotle scribbled on a sheet and tore it off. 'Ask for a chap called Hercules. He's a bit of a moody bugger right now since the Trials began, but he's okay for a god.'

'Right. And where do I go?'

'Oh yes. Augean. You know it? Can't really miss it. Take the number 39 chariot at the stop on the Heraklion road and hop off after the Athens turn. It's second left. You're looking for a stable block with a fair head of cattle and a smell strong enough to make a philosopher recant.'

'Cool. If I do a good job, will there be a permanent place?'

'Probably best you aim to get through the day and take it from there.'

'Right. I'll be going.'

As Tom wandered off, Priastotle drew a line through all his notes under Tom's name and replaced them with "gullible – potential for Senate".

Sink Or Swim: The Choice Is Written In The Stars

Claude Bobbin's lucky break came, he realised, looking back on one gruesomely chilly June Thursday, in year five. His class were on a field trip to Westwitheral and, as part of the "fun"', the whole year group were to be taught bodyboarding.

Claude's experiences of full body immersion in water to that point had been during the weekly humiliation of a swimming class when he and Repson St Mewl -a weedy boy with an already highly developed hypochondria – were bombarded with abuse as they cowered in the shallow end while the teacher, Miss Tansy, checked her makeup and bellowed at them to behave. His parents were part of a small, some might say exclusive, sect of hydrophobic Zoroastrians and discouraged any unnecessary contact with water – what passed for bathtime comprised a prayer for drought and a swift scouring with a dry flannel. Claude's parents fought the requirement for him to undertake swimming lessons with a diminishing enthusiasm and finally decided to allow it when they were promised he would never be expected to actually swim but could stand in the knee-deep water for the forty minutes of the class. Only once did that agreement falter, when Claude slipped on an abandoned sheet of dinosaur knee plasters that Repson had been using as a germ shield, but everyone agreed that no harm had been done and the incident was forgotten.

The parents and the school assumed the same arrangements would apply to the field trip when they noted the need for Claude to take his "swimming togs" but, sadly, or as Claude later saw it, fortuitously, Patrick Oldcolon, the master in charge, who had recently joined the school from teaching woodwork and Etruscan philosophy in a peripatetic young offenders' institution, wasn't informed of the agreement.

'Get in the bloody water, boy,' bellowed Mr Oldcolon with a voice that brooked neither warmth nor compromise.

Claude entered the freezing excuse for fun and stood, shivering as the waves lapped his knees, his body turning the sort of blue usually seen in carbon monoxide poisonings.

'But, sir...'

Individually those words would have had little impact on Patrick but, when articulated by a rather lumpen and malodorous youth, they triggered something base and bestial. Barely containing the rising anger, the teacher strode into the water and, to the astonishment of the class and the understandable terror of Claude, he picked the boy up and tossed him as far as his well-developed guns allowed.

The ensuing silence as Claude described a nearly perfect parabola was counterpointed by the crash and scream as the parabola ended and petrified pupil's plummet to the seabed began. Claude was out of his depth in circumstances where he and his depth were merely remotely acquainted. Mr Oldcolon had thrown Claude beyond the seabed's natural shelf and he sank with the confidence of a granite boulder which, having been freed of the constraints of gravity, is suddenly reacquainted with its powers of attraction.

Many heads turned to the spot where Claude had entered the water, a spot that now rippled with the thoughtless insouciance of a one-year-old that has just peed in his father's eye while said parent changed his nappy. 'Sir, where's Claude?'

In fact, many turned their thoughts to that conundrum. Including Mr Oldcolon, who belatedly bestrode the distance to the point of entry. However, before he could reach the spot, Claude bobbed to the surface, face up, blinking the salt water out of his eyes.

Mr Oldcolon stared as did the class. The teacher stepped forward and, with an expression like that of a naturist who has just found out where the missing cucumber has got to as he sits down for a salad lunch, he discovered the precipitous seabed shelf and disappeared. He, too, reappeared moments later, spluttering and floundering and swam to the shallower waters. Claude meanwhile remained afloat, watching the activity. He did nothing to remain afloat beyond merely being so.

'How are you doing that?'

'Doing what?'

'Not sinking?'

'I don't know. I just am.'

Indeed, Claude was unsinkable. Many boys tried but, coupled with an ability to hold his breath longer than most – a requisite skill he developed as a youngster given his whole family's antipathy to washing – he would bob to the surface long before they had been able to cause him any distress.

Some tried to teach him swimming after that, but they still had to deal with his parents' beliefs and the fact that Claude was a shit swimmer.

And such a newfound skill may have remained a curio of childhood but for an unexpectedly novel sport developed in the salty warm waters of Grand Cay – the International Buoyancy championships. Under encouragement of Mr Oldcolon, who had never forgotten the unsinkable Claude, Claude entered and won all categories. He wasn't typical in terms of physique for a sporting superstar and that won him a small but loyal band of supporters keen to promote sporting success alongside an appalling body image.

When, finally, Claude the Unbeatable as well as Unsinkable brought the world championships back to Britain, they were hosted in Westwitheral where Mr Oldcolon started the first mechanized sink. The whole event was sponsored by St Mewl's Pharmaceuticals, though its CEO and founder, Repson, couldn't attend to give out the prizes as he was halfway through a cycle of thrice daily kale and cardamom enemas that had been prescribed to cure a persistent and wholly imagined eczema caused by the overapplication of dinosaur plasters.

The Bionicist

Eldritch Pomeroy steepled his fingers and released a silent curse. Fortunately for Hildegard Tilt, even now struggling into the seat opposite from the wheelchair, he had had the presence of mind to attach his recently updated "permanently caring" eye-mouth combo, so masking his real feelings at the presence of his most stupid patient.

Hildegard fumbled – the woman was defined by her fumbles, thought Eldritch – for a tissue and dabbed various parts of her face. As much to distract himself from this self-evidently self-pitying performance, Eldritch made a note to have Gerrard, his PA, send her details of the latest in suppurating suppression skins. He was especially gratified at their take up, though the recent reports of unsightly bleaching on those needing a darker skin tone would need to be followed up. Especially after the disaster of his range of "knowing noses", allowing the wearer to choose their most prominent feature to suit the cultural and religious sensitivities of their audience. He shuddered at the memory of the headline: "Beware the racist bionicist's proboscis".

'Oh, Professor, how could I be so silly?'

Eldritch peered at his patient, easily but unwillingly resisting the urge to answer this patently rhetorical question with a brutally honest answer. 'What happened, Mrs Tilt? It's not like they were a pair of spectacles you might forget.'

'Peach mojitos,' she offered by way of a response.

Eldritch prided himself on the depth of his hard-won cynicism. He liked to believe he was capable of unpicking even the most abstruse of answers proffered by his patients. But this defeated him. 'Mojitos?'

To Eldritch's surprise – his left eyebrow performed a passable rumba, leading to an immediate regret that he had omitted adding his static brow-line to his features when he had got ready for his first appointment – Hildegard giggled. She was so unsuited to that action, given that the harmonics of her jowls were clearly aligned, and not in a good way, to the wave pattern caused by the giggle at its peak. He made another note to include with the suppuration suppression skin, a detailed list of the available humour modes she might adopt which would, in a heartbeat, remove the possibility of unsightly jiggles breaking out during laughter.

'I think it's the combination of peach and alcohol. One and I'm Sensual Siren…'

Eldritch winced at the image, sadly acknowledging that the limits of modern-day bionics meant controlling visualisation was a way off.

'But after two I'm insensible.' She shrugged and waved at her hollow trouser legs, which would have been filled with two limbs. 'I was legless. I'd taken off my day pins and had on my party calves – you did them beautifully, Professor, they just melt into my Jimmy Choos.'

He nodded at the compliment. It was the least he deserved.

'But the boys I was with left them behind. I can't go to work wearing my party calves, can I? I'll need some temporary legs to see me through until I can arrange for my own to be retrieved.'

Eldritch pondered this woman with her open face and untroubled countenance, a product of his engineering and medical skills. There were many benefits to being the best bionicist around and having a willing – and rich – client like Mrs Tilt wasn't one of them. 'Mrs Tilt – Hildegard,' the woman simpered – he scratched another note to include the removal of facile features from her next upgrade, 'I am good at what I do. I can provide you with hands for the garden and the gala, arms that can squeeze and seduce, legs that can beguile and beast. You can have an infinite range of faces and fingers. But there are limits.' He held up a hand to forestall any protests and was disappointed to realise there were none coming. 'I cannot provide you with common sense.'

Jobs For The Boys And Bats

'Mr Acula, can I…?'

'Doctor.'

'Sorry?'

'It's Doctor Acula.'

'Oh? Right. Doctor of what?'

'Does it matter?'

'No, I suppose not. I'm just curious.'

'Haematology.'

'Oh, so why…?'

'Why have I applied for this job?'

'Well, yes. I understand the medical side might attract you, but it's a little below your…'

'I enjoy working nights.'

'Yes, your CV says that. It's unusual, what you put.'

'Is it?'

'Will not work days. Most people aren't so prescriptive.'

'My family are committed nocturnals. Not that I'm not flexible.'

'Oh? Good.'

'Yes, I'm happy with sunsets and the occasional sunrise. Oh, and eclipses. I'm good with eclipses.'

'Good to know. Not that we've many of those to worry us. Okay, can you explain what skills you'll bring to the role as dental hygienist?'

'I have an interest in teeth, perfect teeth.'

'Are there such things? I mean, whenever does one see perfection in… Oh yes, well, they are impressive. And so, erm, prominent?'

'I've been complimented on my teeth by many people.'

'Really?'

'Oh yes. You'd be amazed at the number of people who become very excited when they first see my teeth. "My God, look at your teeth!" That kind of thing.'

'No, that doesn't surprise me at all. Any other skills?'

'Well, clearly I'm good with blood. I relish it, in truth, so no silly fainting.'

'Okay.'

'And I can provide a unique anaesthetic option for those scared of needles.'

'Really?'

'Yes. I just smile and… There you go, exactly.'

'Gosh! Yes, well, that was a surprise. Quite overpowering. I'll make a note of your application. Can I just check how we should address you? Do you have a first name?'

'Just stick with Acula. Doctor Acula. But most people run it together. Sort of cutesy nickname, I suppose. Maybe that would work best.'

'Yes, that sounds a good idea. What should I put?'

'Dr Acula. Now it looks like the sunset is nearly done – rather fine, isn't it? I must fly. Busy busy. You know how it is. Places to go, people to see, blood to drink…'

Umbrollia Revisited

Umbrollia was unique in nature, having developed a wormhole between it and its neighbouring parallel universe, through which lonely and lost brollies and umbrellas and other misplaced weather protectors passed, in the hope of finding a more caring environment where they would be remembered even though it had turned out sunny. And, generally, those abandoned parasols and parapluies contented themselves with their new situation which, while not heavily peopled with caring users, at least had eradicated all windowless lost property offices and dank cloakrooms. No spring-loaded rain protector languished for long in the low gravity environment of Umbrollia but spent happy days auditioning for remakes of Mary Poppins and Singing in the Rain, with robotic actors taking the human roles or enjoying a spin class on a windy beach where the experts turned themselves inside out and back again to the astonishment of the recently arrived.

One day, when the forecast squalls had the world's protective apparatus heading for the outdoors, a frisson of excitement rippled through the tight-furled, triple-tipped populous. Word had it that an owner had been seen on the hillside, striding around and muttering about its much loved and lost rainshade. Every time this happened hope soared in the artificially canopied crowds – could it be their old owner cared so much they had made the effort to cross to the next universe in defiance of all natural laws to look for their trusty coverage? Older members of Umbrollia's elite worried he might be some sort of opportunistic trickster, intent on grooming the more vulnerable members of Umbrollia's community, with a view to cruelly selling them a vision of caring new owners and considerate drying facilities, only to flog them on the cheap to the indifferent if inadequately prepared?

After a lot of toing and froing and a fair bit of opening and closing, a delegation of the most robust brollies and bumbershoots, parasols and sunshades was dispatched to inquire of the man's intentions. Umbrellas are naturally silent, so the man didn't see them until he was surrounded. To the watching audience he looked startled when he saw what had approached him.

The leading brolly opened slowly and spoke. It got as far as "good morning", when the man lost all definition as the life drained out of him, the shock of animated weather guards being too much for him to take.

The lead brolly looked at the sunshade representative. 'Well?'

The sunshade looked at the overcast sky and shrugged. 'Looks like he's become a shadow of his old self. He won't be needing us.'

The brolly nodded. 'Shame.'

The parasols watched the brollies go. 'Why do they always put a dampener on things?'

'It's the nature of the beast. Fancy a quick twirl?'

'Why not?'

Day Eight

Terry Godd sat slumped and looked mournfully at the cheery man opposite. 'And?'

Dr Pattison Abraham tapped his fingertips together nervously. 'You need rest.'

'Rest? I can't rest. I've got to finish this commission or...' Terry gasped as pain seared across his lumber region. 'Sheez.'

Pattison moved swiftly to Terry's side. 'Let me see.'

'My back's been playing up since day four. I was promised help with the heavy lifting, but you can't trust a bunch of jobbing primates, can you? Not when they've not been around long. Harry told me to do the big structural stuff last, but I couldn't see how that would work.'

Pattison palpated the affected area while small sparks issued from Terry's ears. 'Harry's your brother?'

'Yes, we Godds do all head office's major projects. Been in the family for ever. Father to son and so on.'

'He's experienced, isn't he?'

'Oh sure, he's been pulling these things together for eons, but this is a biggie.'

'Surely they're all big ones? Can you lean that way? Then that. Then that.'

'You want me everywhere, don't you?'

'You'll get used to it. So, this is special?'

'Yes. See, this one's going to be recorded, right? We've got scribes these days. They'll write it all down.'

'Write? What's that?'

'It's a new technology. In Harry's time he'd put in a shift and sit back, waiting for the adulation and what happens? A couple of generations being revered and then it all fades to some half-baked myth. Usually, the ingrates go off and worship the sun or the moon, or some river or weather system. They don't ask where they came from, do they? Ouch. Bloody hell, doc, careful.'

'Hell? What's that?'

'Ah right, that's another neat innovation, helps keep the clients focused on the Main Man.'

'Who is?'

'In this case it'll be me, natch. When it's finished.'

'You'll enjoy that, will you?'

'If I get it done. The catch is that, according to head office, I have seven days to get this show up and running.'

'Why seven days? Anyway, what's a day?'

'It's the time it takes to build a client base with all the infrastructure… planet, mammal entourage, a range of healthy food snacks, climate varieties to allow for a choice of pigmentations and holidays… Look, can we pick up on that later, okay? I need to meet this publishing deadline. If the first two clients aren't in situ, ready for the launch, with the first couple of chapters written and off to the printers inside seven days, I'm toast. Can you get me back to work?'

'Well, you should take care. You're not that young…'

'Ah, that's just the way I'm imagined – it's the all-knowing wisdom piece we Godds are known for. Means the flowing grey hair, benign and thought-lined countenance and fulsome (also grey) beard come as standard. I need to get through the seven days, top up the oceans and rivers and pop the newly created clients in their garden.'

'Well, I suppose. Can you take a few of these day thingies off afterwards?'

'Hmm, I really need to see them over the first few chapters. I could ask my assistant to keep a watching brief.'

'That would be good.'

'If it goes wrong at the start, there's no knowing where it might end.'

Pattison sat at his desk and wrote a prescription. 'What's the worst that might happen?'

'Oh goodness. Where do I start? Famine, global petulance, daytime television, Morris dancing. They might even want a vote.'

'Yes, well, I hope this assistant is up to it.'

'Oh, me and the snake go a long way back. He'll be fine.' Terry took the prescription and peered at the indecipherable scribbles. 'What am I meant to take?'

'An apple a day. Pretty standard stuff. So, what's this record called? I may get one for the missus for her birthday. Will there be an Audible version?'

'The Bibble and that will depend on how well it goes.'

'I'll just jot that down so she knows what to ask for.'

Resetting To Zero

Amber Trent sits in her chair and focuses on the garden. The wind of earlier has died away and the birds, sated on seeds, are elsewhere. All is still and silent.

Amber Trent doesn't move. She is replete, pain free and alert. Today, her son, Patrick, will visit. His son will marry next year, he has told Amber and he will, she is sure, tell her of the latest plans.

Amber Trent knows the other residents will be having tea later in the communal lounge and that they will be kind and understanding when she sits in the green winged chair.

Amber Trent wants nothing so much as to die. This room, this flat, is her prison, its pleasantly decorated walls and personal knick-knacks reminders of a time when she had choices. Her escape is to the doctor's or the hospital for kind, understanding people to take great care in humiliating her as they hunt for a vein or insert a tube, compassionately extending her life for no purpose beyond the fact they can.

Amber Trent likes her little patch of garden and the insistent birds. But they don't answer her questions and stimulate her like Rodney once did. Patrick and his son, whose name will come to her shortly, are kind and attentive but more absent than present. The residents and warden smile and nod but soon tire of Amber's silence. Rodney used her silence as his backdrop; it created the auditorium for his soliloquys. Now that theatre is hushed, but no longer expectant, and all Amber wants is for the curtain to close.

Amber Trent knows people would wonder at her greatest wish, telling her what she must live for. But they don't see it as Amber sees it. The golden silence that makes up most of her day is, without Rodney, not just the absence of noise but the absence of hope.

Amber Trent is no longer still; her shoulders heave in silent sobs as a single tear slowly wends its way down her cheek.

The Itchy Arse Of Fame

The Sphinx sat, as it had done for centuries, eyeing the horizon with a jaundiced gaze. Which, he thought, was rather appropriate given the puss-yellow cloud of sand that anyone with half a brain could see massing on the far horizon.

He'd been around long enough to know that anthropomorphising the weather would get him the square root of nowhere but, bloody hell, if this didn't happen again and a-bloody-gain. He'd just recovered from the last scouring, been dug out of the resulting dune by willing if less than thoughtful archaeologists and, wouldn't you know it, a bit of low pressure and another bugger of a blast was readying itself to repeat the punishment. It wasn't as if he needed to exfoliate, was it? So, could you blame him for ascribing a malevolent intention to each recurring sandstorm?

As always happened, he began to feel the urge to turn slowly and imperceptibly, so that the smallest part of him faced the on-rushing tumult. He knew from countless other batterings that he'd just have lined himself up when the first psychotic granules would pummel his nethers, wearing down his resistance and filling his rear orifice with yet more sharp custard-coloured dust.

Maybe, he pondered with a misanthropic sigh, he was called the Sphinx because the part of his form that needed the most restoration was his serially abused sphincter.

Or maybe, he wondered, as tonnes of microscopic stone shrapnel ripped across his bows, his name came from the moronic team who'd thought it such a good idea to put one such as he in an effing desert in the first place. After all, they had to be a bunch of complete arseholes, didn't they?

The Sphinx folded his front paws, tucked in his chin and closed his eyes. Who'd be famous, eh?

Surprise Surprise

Penstemon Stromboli peered round the curtain at the UPS man as he struggled up the drive with the package. She didn't recall ordering anything and certainly nothing so large. Though, she thought, as the delivery man checked the label and his little handheld device, what with the ridiculous excess packaging, it wouldn't surprise her to find it was something as mundane as a saucepan, or yet another unnecessary item of clothing that her daughter had purchased.

Penny waited by the door until the man knocked, not wanting to give away how she had been watching him from the moment he climbed out of his van. That curtain twitching was something her mother did, not her. No, she just happened to be looking. That said, there was no reason to give the man an excuse to assume she was that sort of woman. The knock was on the cheery side of confident. As Penny pulled the door open a crack, she was met with the full LED wattage of the serially well-trained courier.

'Hellooo! Am I in the presence of,' the man checked the handheld, 'Delphine Stromboli?'

'No.'

'No?' To say he looked disappointed would be like suggesting puppies enjoy negative reinforcement. 'Oh.'

'She's my daughter.'

'Oh!' Hope restored, the man – Barry Tigger, according to his lapel badge – beamed, 'And would Mother like to accept this package on behalf of her pride and joy?'

Penny hesitated. If this hail and well met fellow knew only a scintilla about her relationship with Della, he would know just how many things were wrong with that question. Reluctantly, she nodded. 'I suppose so. What is it?'

'What…?' Barry leant forward in a sort of conspiratorial way. 'You know, in my job that is the question I ask myself all the time. I mean

ALL. It's what keeps me sane, you know, speculating. I knock at the door and am greeted by a range of humanity. In those few seconds I have with the customer, I can try and assess what exactly they might be ordering. Take you, fr'instance…'

Penny instinctively took a step back. The last thing she needed was this jolly tradesperson deconstructing her personality based on their fleeting acquaintance. Maybe he had seen her behind the curtain. Oh God…

'Clearly you're a sophisticated, well-educated woman with a variety of interests. It could easily be…' Barry's gaze met Penny's and for a second she wanted him to continue, but then sense prevailed.

She pulled the door back. 'Perhaps you'd lean it against the wall.'

He nodded, grateful, she thought, to be relieved of the burden of coming up with something plausible and flattering.

'Can you sign, please? Just your name here.'

She took the slightly tacky device, doing her best to hide the moue of distaste that tickled her lips involuntarily. 'There.' She handed it back and looked at the parcel. To her surprise, Barry hadn't gone as he, too, studied it.

'The label says it's from Clone Co. Maybe Delphine has bought you another daughter.'

Penny felt rather than saw him step away, sure he was smiling, knowing he meant well, knowing she was expected to proffer some sort of witty riposte. But the horror of a second Delphine invading her space, a replica of her selfish, indolent, demanding, draining daughter was too much. She leant back on the door to close it and, as it clicked shut, she slid to the floor, her eyes never leaving the box.

*

Two hours later a key rattled in the lock and Penny rolled away to allow a surprised-looking Delphine to enter.

Delphine dropped her bag and bent to her mother's side. 'You okay?' she asked, with little of the concern others might have expected. 'Why…?'

Delphine's gaze followed her mother's shaky finger. She took a moment to register the package and then a smile gradually grew across her face. 'Ooo, it's come, then?' She stood and hurried through to the kitchen, returning with a knife. With an expertise borne of a life spent shopping online, she sliced open the taping and exposed the inevitable padding.

Penny watched these manoeuvres from her prostrate position. She wanted to say something, to ask why she felt the need to have a sister. What good would come of it? She looked up to see Delphine looming over her.

'What do you think, Mum?'

Penny squinted at the figure that Delphine's delicate disrobing had revealed. Was that Delphine, Mark 2? She coughed and managed to say, 'Why? Why another sister?'

For a moment, Delphine looked surprised, then she laughed, a rolling roistering rollicking sort of laugh that continued as tears formed on her lids. She bent double to try and regain her composure and, as she stood, she reached behind Penny to turn on the light.

Penny gasped. The figure in front of her, a figure that was gradually animating as the charge from the batteries began to work their miracle, wasn't the spitting image of Delphine. No, not even close. The mannequin that in less time than it took Barry to deliver, and which would be alive and waiting to have its software installed any moment, wasn't Delphine; it was Penny. Her daughter had cloned her mother.

Penny turned to look at Delphine still standing over her, still brandishing the knife with which she had removed the packaging. Once again, she asked, 'Why?'

'Why? Because, Mother dear, this,' she waved behind her, 'will be the mother that I've always wanted, the mum I've always deserved.' She took a small step forward. 'The question isn't why, it's what? What are we going to do with you?'

The Gender Neutrality Of Superheroes

Trent "Emojiman" Doublebake pushed the door closed with a smiley face and sighed. His aura rubbed away fake tears and he conjured up a tight toothy smile before entering the kitchen.

Adelaide "Supplegirl" Doublebake unravelled herself from the stretch pole and closed her kindle. 'If that's the best face you can make, I'd guess today wasn't the best?'

Trent forced out a wave that hovered overhead before being replaced by an old man shuttling stage left and a round face crying happy tears. 'We spent the morning trying to decide if the turd emoji should be rainbow coloured to reduce the racist connotations of the original. You'd think the PR people could do that rather than a group of superheroes. We should be out there doing what we do best.'

'Being childish?'

A round face with its tongue out, followed by a single raised finger, preceded Trent's reply, 'We provide a graphic appreciation to societal challenges to improve cultural understating and reinforce society's core values.'

'You make industrial scale faces with your mind to cheer up the serially pissed off.'

'What's got into you? Something's bent you out of shape?'

'No... it's... Millicent found out what her superpower is today.'

Trent stood, full beam emoji enveloping them and party poppers exploding all around. 'That's fantastic. What... she's not a bloody bat, is she? Or a cat? We don't need any more feline fanatics scrabbling over the roof at two in the morning.'

'No, it's useful if a touch... dangerous.'

'Acid girl? Destructor? Her grandpa will be pleased. To say I was a disappointment is an understatement.'

'At least emojis bring in the money. Having a Destructor wreak havoc would cost a fortune.'

'Is she a Destructor?'

'No. Fire Girl.'

'Oh. Okay. A bit retro, but she'll always have work. Especially if she can master colours. Very popular for weddings and bar mitzvahs, not to mention Bonfire Night and July 4th.'

'That's it exactly. Retro. I've tried to bring her up to understand that stereotyping isn't appropriate and then this. It's… it's humiliating. How can I face the girls?'

Trent's bubble put a finger to its chin and waited. Adelaide wrapped her arms around herself several times and gave herself a firm hug. 'She had a notification and downloaded the powerapp. I was wringing out the washing and became rather tied up. Took me a while to untangle myself and when I did, she was already showing off to Dolomite next door.'

'It's what teenagers do. You must remember when you got yours?'

'Yes, but back then it came in the post with a book of instructions. My dad wouldn't let me at it until he'd read it all through. I'd almost stretched to breaking point by the time he let me at the kit. Still, it didn't seem too bad and she was so excited I grabbed my phone to record her. She was sparking.'

'I wish I'd been here.'

'That's why I wanted to record it. Here…' Adelaide held up her phone.

Trent flicked through the images, his bubble of delight slipping to hand-slapped-over-the-mouth horror. 'She immolated the neighbour?'

'Technically, but the Johnsons are all Relifers and her mum soon had her melted bits back in shape. I think the only permanent scarring is to the petunias. No, look…'

'I don't… Oh, I see! She fires pink.'

'Exactly. We're meant to be progressive superheroes and what do we get? A Fire Girl whose base flames are all pink. I ask you. I bend over backwards - '

'All ways…'

'Thank you… and all the suppliers do is provide this. I mean, even you're trying to bring your emojis into the new century and we get lumbered with Girl Fawkes. It's enough to make you weep. No, Trent, stop that. I've only just done the kitchen floor and I don't need to sop up your thought-tears just now.'

A Life In The Day

'So, Albertine Mayfly, any moment now it will be dawn on your Big Day and -'

'My only day.'

'Well, that's true but…'

'Though I suppose that's merely the average, so some mayflies may pop their clogs earlier and some go on to day two. That would be something.'

'True, but our viewers are hoping for a really Big Day for you, Bertie. Can I call you Bertie?'

'I suppose. I mean, I've only been up and about for an hour or so and I've not had much time to think about diminutives, what with hair and makeup calls, the -'

'Hair?'

'Well, strictly it was wing tints, curlers for the proboscis and some antennae crimps, but that's a bit of a mouthful.'

'Quite. So, as we count down to dawn on this fiery morn, what -'

'That's very good. Rhyming dawn with morn. Was that scripted or spontaneous?'

'Scripted.'

'Oh. Well, still, well done to who thought of it. Who was it?'

'Jason.'

'Go, Jas!'

'Can we get back to your plans for Your Day? That's why the Spring Watch Live! audience will be tuning in. How do you intend starting off?'

'Well… and Jas would approve I'm sure… I've not had much time to think about it…'

'Okay.'

'But I thought I might have a go at painting.'

'Painting?'

'Well, yes. After all, this sunrise is sublime, isn't it? I've never seen one like it.'

'No, well, you wouldn't have, would you?'

'Oh, very droll. Yes, if I can capture this abundant radiance…'

'Aren't you being a touch optimistic?'

'Why? Oh gosh, is it going to rain? I'd not thought about that.'

'No. I mean, I don't know what the weather holds. I was thinking how hard painting will be for you… a mayfly.'

'I know I've not had many lessons…'

'Any.'

'Exactly.'

'And you have feet designed to grip stalks.'

'Now, I talked that through with Sharon – lovely girl, if a touch orange.'

'Who's Sharon?'

'Well, she's Jas' squeeze… Aww, don't they make a nice couple? Anyway, she did my makeup and she said she knows this really good guy, very reasonable, out Romford way, who's done her boobs and butt and says he could easily fix me up with a couple of digits and opposable thumbs by lunchtime. So, I'm booked in.'

'Plastic surgery?'

'Corporeal enhancements. He's going to retint my wings at the same time.'

'You can't spend your whole day under the knife just to squeeze in a quick daub by the time you're done. It's not natural.'

'Oh, I see. You want to stereotype me, do you? Burden me with all your mammalian prejudices. You expect me to buzz about, find a mate, shag them on some stalk while you film us at it, give birth to a few eggs and snuff it. Do you know how much energy loss that shagging involves? If I skip that part, I've a better than evens chance of enjoying a day two.'

'But that's how you're designed. That's not stereotyping, that's the natural order.'

'Oh, get you. If we're playing the natural order game, you should be out hunting and gathering and your missus nurturing, rather than you posing in front of a camera while she's enjoying a sweaty hour of downward facing dog to Seb's upward pointing polecat at her yoga class.'

'How do you know that?'

'Sharon told me. The point is, it's alright for you to move on, spend your day ordering your people about, but not me. I'm to remain forever stuck doing the same old same old. Well, wise up, Bub. We're taking control over our lives. No more of this temporal hegemony fixing me to a day's action, no more of this May Fly. From now on, it's Will Fly, where I want and when I want.'

'Have you finished?'

'Yes, I suppose.'

'And did you read the contract?'

'Contract?'

'The bit where it commits you to acting as directed.'

'No…'

'Didn't your agent explain?'

'I haven't had time to hire an agent.'

'That's because you've wasted all your time with Sharon. Look, the sun is up. Just fly over to the pond and check out the talent.'

'Does it say I have to shag?'

'No, but you'd be the first not to.'

'And if I make it to day two, could I maybe have a go at painting?'

'I'll raise it with the team. Okay?'

'Oh alright.'

'And there he goes, embracing his one Big Day…'

'Unless I make it through…'

'Following the paths laid down by his ancestors over millennia.'

'Unless I get to do some painting…'

'And now we will take a short break. When we come back, we'll take time to study the fascinating reproductive cycle of the mayfly.'

'Pervert.'

The Triangulation Of Superheroes

'Hi, Bat, you okay to take a call?'

'Who is it, Alfred?'

'The Mayor of Gotham. Sounds a bit angsty.'

'He's always angsty. Put him on.'

The Bat smoothed his cape and noticed a tear with annoyance. You just couldn't get a decent cape these days. A couple of conflagrations, maybe a small Armageddon and pfft! You're off to Bat About Town again.

'Hi,' the Bat recognised the nasal congestion that distinguished the mayor from the normally aspirated. 'That you, Batman?'

'Mr Mayor? How's Gotham? My spies tell me it's still predominantly crime free and peaceful.'

'Indeed so.'

The Bat waited and then said, 'I sense a "but" coming…'

'Better than a butt kicking.' The speaker laughed, then coughed and finally, rather too obviously, spat. It was a different voice but another familiar one.

'You on the line, too, Chief Blue? My lucky day. How can I help Gotham's finest?'

'Well…' The mayor hesitated and the Bat tapped his gloved hand on his rippling thighs.

'Shall I go first, Chief?'

'It's you who's got the problem, Mayor.'

'It's everyone's problem, Chief.'

'I think it really is yours.'

The Bat began to interrupt when the mayor said, 'Look, Batman, it's the peace bit. That's the issue.'

'How so, Mr Mayor? It's what you always wanted. You made it plain you'd done with constant battles on your streets and in your skies and, if I couldn't bring about peace, then you'd have to downgrade my bat-rating – there was some talk of bringing in other Avengers.'

'That was never serious, Batman, and, anyway, you did what we asked, that's true. Only it's no use.'

The chief made a sort of snorting noise. 'It's great. C'mon, Mayor, admit it. Since the Bat finished his contract and moved on, all the misbegotten misfits who'd inhabited the sewers and junk yards and alleys have gone, too.'

'Exactly,' said the mayor, 'and now you're fat and living the good life. Look, it's been fine for you and yours, cruising about, looking good, but tourism's down, hospitals are closing and the construction industry is barely functioning. Throw in the closures of hardware stores, gunsmiths, gentlemen's Lycra outfitters, car repair shops, rocket boot makers and spotlight silhouette artists… and you name it, we're struggling. We had a Bat-based economy and now we have a business mutiny ready to explode.'

Batman sighed. He'd warned them. 'I'm sure your economy will rebalance itself. Given time.'

'Exactly,' said the chief. 'Time.'

'That's precisely what I don't have, Chief Blue. If I was you, I'd enjoy your indolence, because it could be coming to a brutally short ending. If Arianna Dove pips me in the upcoming election, she'll get rid of you as fast as ever the Bat did for the Cat. She's commissioned a poll that purports to show the only reason there was so much crime here was because Batman was here. Her take is Batman was just setting himself up to be shot down, so he could then do the shooting down, and so on. And all the conspiracy theorists are saying I profited from all those growth businesses.'

'Well, you did, Mayor.' The Bat felt tired. He hated politics.

'That's not the point, Batman. Can you help?'

The Bat flicked open his contacts list. 'I can give you a number.'

'But I called you on the hotline. I kept it going just in case.'

'You don't need me in Gotham. Call this number, tell them I gave you their number and explain, and they'll soon have things back in order.'

'Who am I calling?' The mayor sounded suspicious.

'The Joker. He coordinates all the criminals and crackpots. He'll sort out some unpleasant crime and, once I get the call, I'll come and clean things up.'

There was a short silence before the chief said, 'It was before my time, Batman, when you first appeared, but this isn't how it worked then, is it?'

The mayor spoke before the Bat could reply. 'Sometimes, Blue, you say the silliest things.'

Taking Dictation

'Morning, Moses.'

'Morning, God. Looks like it might turn out nice.'

'You fishing for a hint? You had a flutter on a sunny one, have you?'

'God. How could you think such a thing?'

'Hmm. And the fam? The missus happy?'

'She wants more children.'

'Ah yes, that is often the case.'

'You couldn't, you know, maybe work the oracle?'

'How do you mean?'

'Now, don't get all sturm and drang, but word has it you're not ill-disposed to a little IC.'

'IC?'

'Immaculate conception. You know, bonk-free babies. Might save my back.'

'No comment.'

'So, it's true.'

'Look, Moses, I've warned you about reading ahead. When we decided to write it down, we told everyone not to read ahead. You'll have to sort out your family issues yourself.'

'Oh great. It's okay for your lot, divine favours regularly bestowed, but when a mate – who, let's face it, hasn't ever let you down – asks for an itsy-bitsy piece of benign, divine intervention, he's told he's on his own.'

'Moses, let's not get too far ahead of ourselves, shall we? I'm the Supreme Being, capiche? The maker of all things, the all-seeing, the all-knowing -'

'Not a mate, then?'

'Not a mate.'

'Great. So, what brings you through the clouds, oh Supremo? I hope it's not another of your hikes. Do you know how many sandals I wore out getting that lot around the Red Sea?'

'You don't half whinge, don't you?'

'You try walking round that sodding pond with a bunch of miserable ingrates.'

'Careful. I can always find somewhere for you to reflect on your lot.'

'Oh yes. Why don't you send me to the desert for forty days and nights? Like you do -'

'I told you just now about reading ahead. More of that and it'll be forty years, not forty days.'

'You'd never?'

'Try me. Now, focus. I'm here because I've a job for you.'

'Why does that fill me with the joys? Not.'

'Oh, get over yourself. You're not that important, matey-boy. There are plenty of others who could do your job. Abraham, Noah, Job…'

'Fine. I get the picture. All I'll say is just you wait until your next 360-degree appraisal. I'll have a few pointers to suggest about your management style, believe you me.'

'Yada yada yada… Look, do you want this job or should I…?'

'Yes, alright. You know I've got a family and contraceptives aren't cheap.'

'They don't exist.'

'They don't? What about that scallop poultice?'

'Useless.'

'Sulphur embalming?'

'Unpleasant but about as useful as a pointless parable.'

'Figgy unguent? Orange pip insets? Date pate?'

'You're a sucker for a new idea, aren't you?'

'Bloody hell. Wait till I get my hands on that Ham. He'll be lucky if he can -'

'That's exactly why I've called. This defaulting to violence when things don't go your way.'

'He got me sticking sodding pips up my pee-pee.'

'One might question the credulity of the man who thinks stippling his wife's fanny… Though, when you think about it, that may be a sure fire - excuse the pun - way to slow down her enthusiasm for procreation…'

'Oh yes, have a good laugh. What is it, then?'

'Oh yes. Right. Now, here's the thing. I think the people need a bit of a nudge. I'm not sure they've got the "One God" piece yet. They're still inclined to offer up sacrifices to all sorts of dodgy deities and second-rate celestials. So, I thought we might sketch out a few suggestions for how we take things forward.'

'Uh huh?'

'You don't sound sure.'

'No, it's got its attractions.'

'But…?'

'It's all a bit, you know, egalitarian. More Jonny than Jehovah.'

'What do you suggest? Recommendations?'

'Better.'

'Rules…?'

'More like it.'

'Commandments?'

'Now you're talking.'

'Won't they think I'm a bit pushy?'

'You're God, not some carpet seller. They expect to be told. They can wait a bit for the free will piece.'

'Have you read part two? It's not for you to…'

'I may have had a sneaky peek… It needs work though.'

'How do…? No, I told you what I think about reading ahead. So, okay, let's go with commandments. I've a few suggestions and -'

'How many?'

'Twenty-seven.'

'Oh, no no no. Maximum ten, five for preference.'

'Ten?!'

'Maybe we should run through them.'

'Run through them? I thought you said they should be commandments. You know, sort of The Imposed Dictates of the All-Knowing?'

'Yes, well, that's good in theory, of course, but you'll want to have a focus group to test the reactions across an appropriate demographic.'

'I don't know…'

'Fr'instance, there's been a certain amount of chatter about you embracing recycling.'

'I'm sorry?'

'Well, see, here's the thing. In the good ol' days, you, being God, would decide it's time to create Heaven and Earth and all that good stuff. Right? Chapter one, yes?'

'Yes…'

'And then you'd run the cycle and reach Armageddon… Yes, I know that's reading ahead, but bear with me.'

'I'm listening.'

'So, the thinking has it, this can't be the only building project you've been involved in. I mean, if this one's finite, there must have been others. And there will be more to come? Am I warm?'

'In a manner of speaking, though, of course, it isn't always Heaven and Earth… I like to mix it up.'

'Natch. What was the last one?'

'Tupperware and Clingfilm. It didn't really catch on. Too ephemeral. Hence the rock and the hard place shtick.'

'Exactly, all that plastic.'

'How'd you know about plast -'

'I'm the bloody prophet, God. It's what I do.'

'Right, yes. Soz. On you go.'

'What people want, if there are going to be these Commandments, is an emphasis on recycling. You know, reusing the old structures. If you make people sort through their rubbish, bin it properly, then things will last longer and we'll not bugger things up for the future generations.'

'Bit pointless, don't you think?'

'Sorry?'

'Well, since you've had a peep at the last chapter, you know things end. Armageddon, yes?'

'We did wonder if we might have a word about that.'

'I can hardly change it now.'

'Oh, come on, you could rewrite the ending. There's sure to be a second edition of the Bible. How are the sales?'

'Bit disappointing, in truth. Though there's this Gibbon who says he can guarantee me one in every inn.'

'Bit of a risk, lining yourself up with a primate. Not great PR when you've made man the big dog around here.'

'I'll get him to change his name. Anyway, no changes. I don't buy these happy endings.'

'I thought Tolkien nailed it with the Grey Havens.'

'Pah! Bloody fantasist. Time of men, indeed. Come on, we've drifted off the commandments. What else?'

'Hang on, where's my list? Right. Compulsory veganism, early adoption of democracy, soaps to have credible plot lines, no one to invent the mullet or the beehive and equality for women.'

'You what?'

'I told them it wouldn't fly. Let's park that one. Maybe if there's a second edition. What about you? What's on your list?'

'People can only worship me, I am the one true God, no false idolatry –'

'You don't think that's says "me me" a little too much? It does suggest a lack of confidence, don't you think?'

'What do you suggest?'

'Religious tolerance as a minimum. Or, if that's a bit too next millennium for you, we could scrap religion and encourage glee clubs. Everyone likes a bit of a singalong.'

'Moses, I think you're rather missing the point. Just grab a chisel and I'll dictate my ten.'

'There you go. "Dictate". It'll all go horribly wrong if all you want are a bunch of yes people doing your bidding, saying how wonderful you are. All that adulation isn't good for a god.'

'Well, let's give it a whirl, eh? If it's a total balls-up, I'll know the next time I do a Heaven and Earth combo. You ready?'

'Chisel poised…'

The Wisdom Of Carp

The Sage of Upyaws lowered himself onto his fishing stool and sighed a tired sigh. Another beautiful day, a glorious view, a lake full of willing carp. He sighed again and picked up the Tupperware box, unclipping the lid and peering inside. Egg and cress. Could be worse – could be ham and tomato, though they weren't as bad as tuna and cucumber. That was the pits. Not the sort of fayre a Sage should be offered.

'Hello?'

Christ, not already? He looked at his watch. Two minutes past nine. 'Bit bloody early.'

'I'm sorry?'

'To be badgering me. Most of you buggers wait until half past.'

'I really am sorry, but what are you talking about?'

The Sage dragged his rheumy gaze away from the mellifluous cloud formations and peered at his interrogator. He fitted the mould: neat hair, ironed shirt, clean jeans, super keen expression, one of those ridiculous male scents. 'You'll be wanting my thoughts.'

'Well,' the young man shifted his weight and the Sage wondered if he was about to break into a dance – there was that couple from Whitstable who'd paid homage with an unnecessarily overvigorous foxtrot; she was pretty good, but he looked like he was in the process of passing a hedgehog, 'that's a very generous offer.'

'Yeah, tell me about it.' He stretched his back. 'I blame the Bugle. They said I did it for the love of it. Sods.'

The young man did his best to look interested but couldn't stifle a yawn.

The Sage noticed things like that, evidence of a lack of respect. 'Oh, that's lovely. You come here, disturb my peace and then yawn like

I'm the one who's boring. Well, thank you, but if you think I'm going to help you…'

The young man shook his head like a small sliver of brain was caught up in the wiring and its presence made thinking incoherently unnecessarily difficult. 'I'm here to help you.'

'You?! Help me?! Oh, that's rich.' He peered more closely. The man looked like he was a trainee undertaker. 'So, come on. What's your best shot? This'll be peachy.' He waved vaguely at the gymnastic confusion that was the cloud bank. 'Where do you get your insights, then? Probiotic moss? Avocado infused ley lines? Some fancy New Age bollocks, I'll be bound.'

If the aggression surprised the young man – and the way he swayed like he was a badly tethered goat in a typhoon indicated that might be the case – he rallied impressively. He opened his man-bag and extracted a dog-eared pamphlet. 'From here, if you must know.'

The Sage squinted at the flimsy booklet and scoffed. 'Oh, don't tell me, you're a Worthy, are you? It's all doing good works and giving them the promise of tea and slippers if they chant some pseudo-baloney thrice weekly and pay the stipend. Charlatans, the lot of you.'

If the young man felt any sense of his being the good guy here it was evidently fast slipping away. It may have been his instinct to calm the Sage as he put a hand on the man's shoulder.

The Sage could barely credit what was happening. If this young shaver had read the article in the Bugle – and everyone must have by now, the Sage was certain – he'd know that you didn't touch him. He'd made that clear. It confused and drained him, being manhandled by those seeking insights and solace from the Wisest of the Wise. Him. He focused all his energy on His Righteous Ire but, in doing so, he stood up too quickly, lost his footing and slipped down the bank into the shallows of the lake. Now he was a foot or two below the cretin, this mock-seer, this fraud and it made him feel like he'd lost both the real and moral high ground.

The youngster raised his hands, palms down, indicating, or so it seemed, that he intended pacifying the rising fury of the damp, muddy aggressor but, due to the differential height, the gesture was more redolent of a religious leader blessing the devout.

The Sage took a deep breath. 'I have come to this sodding lake for twenty-seven years to fish. For the last twenty-five it has been my privilege to share my years of wisdom with whoever decides to join me. I've made people's fortunes, saved lives, repaired damaged relationships, cured the world's malaises, all through the power of my insights. And then you turn up, all M&S chinos and a splash of Simper by Tommy Hilfiger and try and usurp me. How bloody dare you? How could you?' He was nearly in tears.

The young man looked as if he felt awful. He took a step forward, but all that did was cause the Sage to jump back and fall over into the water again.

The youngster looked defeated. 'I'm sorry, but I only wanted to let you know the lake's owners have decided you need a licence to fish and I wanted to make sure you knew.' He pointed further down the bank, to a stool and a net. 'That's me.' He tapped his chest. 'Colin.'

The Sage tried to focus. 'You're not a Sage?'

Colin shook his head. 'I'm not any sort of herb. I work in a tinsel factory. This is my annual leave. I just thought you might not have seen the notices or this booklet of rules, being as you're so busy and I didn't want you to have any hassle.'

The Sage looked at his broken stool, his ruined clothes, his prized rod that was even now floating towards the weir. 'Yeah, well, thanks.' He stood up. 'You don't, you know, want any of my insights?'

Colin scratched his chin and then brightened. 'Where's the best pitch to catch the carp?'

The Sage scrabbled up the bank and righted his stool. 'Here. And I ain't moving. Now, sod off.'

If You Go Down To The Woods Today

If Jerome Corbel needed inspiration, and lately he'd needed a lot, his allotment was his go to happy place. But Donald McJohn was a persistent little bugger and when he said, 'Walk with me,' even suggesting you were worried that your cabbages weren't red enough didn't cut it as an excuse.

Indeed, Jerome thought, just mentioning his allotment these febrile days seemed to put Donald on edge. Take yesterday. All he'd said was he needed to check on how the leeks were faring and Donald had gone all Gulag on him.

And now this walk.

Donald strode ahead, chuntering about tea and conspiracies while Jerome took in the isolation, the chilly air, the sense of something big in the offing. This place was magical. Was Donald going to make some startling revelation? Had he found the genie they were after? He'd lost himself in enough bottles, so you'd think he'd find one occupied by a wish-fulfilling spirit.

Donald was a short man, prone to wear a suit even out here. He stopped abruptly and pointed. 'I wanted you to be the first to know.'

'Know what?'

'The money. There is an answer.'

Jerome looked up, expecting to see the sky filled with pies.

'No, there.' Donald pointed at a Christmas tree.

'Is that the money tree you promised?'

'Better. It's a gem fir. Just shake it and you'll have enough precious stones to buy everything we've ever wanted.'

'That's probably a bit extreme, though…' Jerome tapped his teeth, which felt more rabbit than was entirely comfortable, 'it does mean I was right all along. With my slogan.'

'How's that?' Donald took a quick sip of refined capitalist from his hip flask.

Jerome stepped forward and tapped the pine, ducking as rubies cascaded around his feet. 'As I keep saying, if only you'd listen. For the money, knock the yew.'

The Ballad Of Dennis And Prudence

Dennis Spleen was a quiet man. He was the deputy librarian at Scowle on Nadge's municipal learning centre, a passionate if largely anonymous member of the congregation of the Volcanic Church of the Spiritually Unbound and an avid collector of Victorian Antimacassars, with a particular passion for the Barnsley Panwallop Doilley style that was popularised by Dorothea Gutterbind in her revolutionary work on otherworldly visitations, 'The Bindings of the Nadges'. Dennis was secretly proud, therefore, to be asked to give the annual Gutterbind Tribulation at the WI hall, focusing on the spiritual importance of antimacassars in the development of the Church and the cleanliness of society in general.

What Dennis didn't know was the reason for the invitation. Nor what would happen that night.

Prudence Formica had spent fifty-two years in thrall to her charismatic and controlling mother, Regina. When Regina's heart gave out during a particularly tasty and beguiling rant at the temerity of a Lib Dem counsellor coming to canvas on her doorstep that lasted forty-one minutes without a pause, everyone assumed it was a tragedy. But Prudence was secretly delighted. Ever since she had visited the library, prior to its rebrand as a learning centre, to return her mother's weekly diet of Barbara Cartland novels, she had harboured a secret longing to know the quiet and oddly hirsute deputy librarian, Dennis, better.

She secretly canvassed colleagues for details of his personality ("not sure he has one"), favourite foods ("anything beige really") and hobbies ("there's the swimming thing…").

It was the last one that set in train the events that became known as the Great Nadge Exposure.

At school little went right for Dennis and, while he wasn't especially bullied, he excelled at remaining invisible. That was until year five when a sports teacher, who had not noticed Dennis for six terms, bumped into him on the edge of the pool and sent him in an approximate parabola into the water. No one, least of all Dennis, knew what would happen next, but it turned out he had an instinctive if idiosyncratic ability to swim. Or perhaps an inability to sink would describe it better since, in sporting terms, Dennis found forward propulsion almost impossible.

Dennis enjoyed being in water, but this lack of a stroke embarrassed him. And so it was that he had just reached his thirty-fifth year before he tried open water swimming. It was a rash attempt to be sociable with a new graduate recruit that had seen him join in the swimming party, having received a promise that actually swimming wasn't necessary if he didn't want to. It was as he was happily floating that something large and crepuscular emerged from the depth of the lake causing him to be so startled, he made to withdraw from this presence. While the others studied what turned out to be the remains of a peripatetic Victorian escapologist, whose latest trick had proved one too many, Dennis panicked and attempted to put as much distance between himself and the self-composting corpse. In so doing, he discovered that, while moving forward was beyond him, swimming backwards was as natural as breathing and over-masticating his food.

Soon enough, he was perfecting his reverse swimming in as many of the county's pools and ponds as he could get to. He discerned two things: firstly, Nadge Water was easily his preferred location and second, his swimming was vastly improved by being undertaken in the buff.

The first time Prudence followed him to watch his ritual – a cool Saturday in April – she was initially shocked and then pleasantly flushed at the sight of his hairy buttocks creating a rather extraordinary "W" wave as he ploughed up and down Nadge Water.

Over the following months Prudence followed Dennis' progress. One day, when the sun was particularly glorious, she snapped an image of the still water and the small bobbing figure of Dennis. She knew then she was in love, and she knew she needed to display that love to her hero.

Using contacts of her mother, she manipulated and manoeuvred the WI and Church until Dennis had been invited to give the annual talk. She then prevailed upon the committee to thank him, not in the traditional manner of an overvigorous and tuneless rendition of Jerusalem on the portable zither and a basket of Miriam Proboscis' fruit and jeroboam scone, but with a huge square cake that was rolled onto the dais after Dennis had accepted the desultory applause. Dennis was prevailed upon to cut the confection, whereupon Prudence emerged clad only in a rare and original example of a Rutland loose knit antimacassar that left little to the imagination, while a screen behind them played a short film of Dennis carving a figure of eight on the Nadge.

If Prudence misjudged the audience, and the number of defibrillations undertaken on the committee who were seated in the front row and able to discern the details of the film would suggest she had, she was correct in how her performance was received by Dennis. He was stunned, so much so that Prudence had him parcelled up and slipped into her car. He awoke to find her still immodestly clad in her antique garb and ready to feed him puréed cauliflower cheese and mashed potatoes. He took a mouthful and swooned. Life was indeed good.

If In Doubt Build A Rockery

It is often assumed that, in the world of the Celestial, everything is perfect. There's God and then there are angels. But, for every St Peter and his border controls, there is Gabriel and his defence forces and Michael and his transport brief. There are seraphs and archangels and so on. There is, in short, a pecking order, a hierarchy. And once you've sifted through the original angels, the early and latter-day saints, the goody two shoes who make their way through the induction and citizenship exams, there are still those who aren't recognised, whose presence is mostly tolerated, usually ignored and sometimes disparaged, but without whom Heaven wouldn't function.

When Heaven is booming, religious take up is high and the queues at the Gates stretch back beyond morning, with the inevitable shortage of harp strings and gold quills, there is pressure on the sub-angelic cohorts to do their thing. Clouds need building, nectar grown and refined and togas stitched and cleaned. But if gloom descends and waves of secularism wash over the flocks, the take up of places is reduced to a trickle and unregulated budget-spectres organize group deaths to try and bump up the numbers. It is then the attention of the now underemployed angels drifts to the cohorts and questions are asked. Are there too many? Should there be tougher controls? Should entrants be sponsored by a saint or disciple? Should they be sent to the other place? Indeed, occasionally, the grumblings are so bad there have been discussions around Heaven seceding from the multitudes, cutting the ingrates free to wallow in their mortality without even the merest soupçon of a hope of an afterlife. Heaven, after all, is a finite resource and it has always been understood that the entry requirements should be stiff. The sub-angelic, who pass through, unhindered by issues of past behaviour and future repentance, are an easy target.

One such was Sub-Angel Colin. He was the happy clappy sort, who saw himself as lucky to be helping these beautiful supernatural beings provide their angelic services. He attended daily work allocation and accepted whatever was offered: cloud inflating for the more comfortably formed angels, queue management at the main gates and, occasionally, working with the flocks of heavenly birds, whose feathers were farmed for quills. But, today, the archangels were away at a conference, St Peter had a meeting with the builders about the delays to the new beatific system of checks and balances and the angel handing out roles seemed disinclined to put Sub-Angel Colin forward for anything. Colin didn't despair; it wasn't in his nature. He drifted away, thinking he might find a tub of sunshine and go and spread it on several levels of the unworthy, when a voice, familiar from the Heavenly broadcasts but never before directed at him, boomed.

'COLIN.'

Colin checked. No one else seemed to have heard a thing, so this Godcall must be for him.

'Sir?'

'IT'S JUST GOD, COLIN. YOU DON'T NEED TO BE FORMAL. WE LIVE IN ENLIGHTENED TIMES, YOU KNOW? EVERYTHING'S UNIVERSAL THESE DAYS. ARE YOU FREE? I'VE A JOB.'

'Yes. Of course. Anything.'

'THING IS, I'VE ANOTHER COMMISSION, BIT OF A QUICKIE. A WHOLE WORLD AND EVERYTHING IN IT IN SEVEN DAYS.'

'Goodness. That's a tall order. But I'll do my best.'

'IT'S ALRIGHT. I CAN DO THE WORLD BUILDING THING, BUT I'M GOING TO NEED A GARDEN, A SORT OF HOLDING AREA WHILE THE INHABITANTS ARE PROCESSED. YOU UP FOR THAT?'

'Inhabitants? Oh, what sort? Grottles? Ploins? I heard you'd given up on Scuttlebuckets because of the emissions.'

'THIS IS A NEW ONE, A BIT UNTESTED, BUT THERE'S A LOT RIDING ON IT.'

'Well, we can all do with the work and it's always exciting when you launch a new model. Can you give me a hint? Multiminded gas cloud? Gelloidal Dipthogists?'

'IT'S QUITE THE THING, MORE POST-LIFE THAN ANYTHING. BASICALLY, THEY'RE BIPEDAL CARBON-BASED APES WITH LARGE BRAINS, FEW INHIBITIONS AND A TENDENCY TO INVENT STUPID WAYS OF KILLING THEMSELVES.'

'Oh. Sounds rather retro to me. Still, you're the all-seeing, all-knowing omniporous -'

'DON'T YOU MEAN OMNIPOTENT?'

'Do I? Anyway, you decide.'

'I HAVE. YOU DO THE GARDEN AND WHEN THEY ARRIVE, YOU KEEP THEM AMUSED UNTIL THEIR TRANSPORT HAS BEEN MADE READY. IS THAT UNDERSTOOD?'

'Any particular format?'

'OH, A STANDARD EDEN I THINK, NOTHING TOO FANCY.'

Colin flicked through the Basic Manual For Garden Making until he found Eden. 'Can it have a rockery? It says it's optional.'

'I SUPPOSE.'

'And fruit trees? Is this one to have fruit trees?'

God pondered.

'Maybe peaches? Peaches are always popular…'

'APPLES. LET'S HAVE APPLES.'

Colin could barely contain his excitement. He laboured for days and nights and those little spaces in between, which no one really understands but are often quite romantic and colourful. If he wasn't sure, he asked Kevin, who'd built gardens in the past. 'Make them soothing and calming. They'll be innocents. Strictly no sharp thorns and stones and a few large leaves…'

'Leaves?'

'You said there were to be apples?'

'He insisted.'

'Then you'll need leaves. Trust me.'

When God delivered them, He and Colin watched as the two innocents began exploring. Colin wondered at their wobbly and dangly bits. Maybe God rushed them; seven days was always tight.

God coughed. 'I NEED TO DASH. MRS GOD AND I ARE HOSTING AN IRONIC BARBECUE AND LUCIFER'S PROMISED TO DO HIS SURPRISE ROAST. I NEED TO MAKE SURE IT ISNT GABRIEL AGAIN.'

'Is Mr Luci coming up?'

'I KNOW. THE BASEMENT CARETAKER HERE! ONE HAS TO BE OPEN-MINDED. I'LL BE BACK MONDAY…'

'What's Monday?'

But he was gone.

Kevin came to keep Colin company, bringing his pet snake, Cyril. They watched the innocents eat apples, go very pink, stare at each other's dangly and wobbly bits and run off looking for leaves.

'It won't end well,' he said forlornly.

'Never mind,' answered Colin. 'At least I got to build a rockery.'

Singing Till The Sky Screams

Harrison Harris pulled at the straps of his overalls and sucked on his pipe. 'Nasty,' he opined.

Mrs Jepson-Soffit folded her arms tighter across her chest; causing her bosoms to wonder, not for the first time, if they had chosen the right location to hibernate. 'Mr Harris, I did not call you for a value judgement but merely to tell me why I have a crack in my sky and what you can do about it.'

Harrison sucked harder and winced. The cold air that was already pouring through the firmamental fissure appeared to have overwhelmed the warming properties of his tobacco and caused icicles to form on his oesophagus. 'Do you have a taper?'

'I'm sorry, Mr Harris, but why on earth would I possess a non-indigenous pig-like quadruped in North Yorkshire and, even if I did, why would I give it to you?'

'A taper, you know - the thing you use to light the gas, not a bloody tapir?' Harrison breathed in deeply but carefully, trying to avoid doing any more damage to his internal organs. 'Madam?'

'No, I do not. I don't approve of pipes, not since my husband Roddick accidentally impaled Maestro Godwit, who was trying to perform the Heimlich manoeuvre on him during his antepenultimate hiccoughing fit in the autumn of '17. The poor man had his repertoire severely compromised as a result. What about my sky?'

Harrison tried to keep calm, but he could feel the freeze spreading to his larynx. 'What did you do?'

'Is that relevant? One minute the sky was satisfactorily overcast, the next that split had appeared and the weather had become incorrigibly inclement. I have guests coming in,' she consulted her wristwatch, 'forty minutes and they are expecting to be royally entertained, not cryogenically embalmed. What can you do?'

'Were you planning an al fresco opera, by any chance? Only we've had a few climatic contrafabulations recently, what with genetically modified sopranos competing to bring the house down, only it's gone a bit far.'

Mrs Jepson-Soffit shuffled her substructure and sighed. 'Geraldine, Roddick's eldest by the first violin, entered X Factor and wanted a couple of enhancements. She rather overdid it.'

Harrison was already moving towards his van. He stood on the bumper and pulled off the ladders. 'I'll have a quick squizz and see if I can staple the stratosphere together. Just a temporary solution, of course, but you'll be able to have your soirée with a few additional blankets and some napalm bottom warmers. These things often fix themselves anyway. Low pressure over the Chindits, coupled with an effervescence of cocoa in the Maltings and you'll never know anything was amiss. Though I'd recommend you fit a double-trenchable silencer to your stepdaughter in future.'

'Thank you. I'm most grateful.'

'No problem, though if you could see about that taper, I'd be very grateful. I think my epiglottis is packing up to go somewhere warmer.'

'Oh, don't worry, Mr Harris. My body parts are always deserting me. Why, only last week my anus handed in her notice. Apparently, she feels neglected and wants to work for someone more discerning. It's the third this year and quite frankly, I'm fed up having to hold myself. Now, a schooner of sherry before you go about your work?'

If Only…

Hieronymus Hampton settled behind the ancient desk and rubbed a cautious finger across the much-scored beading. So many great men and a few women had sat here, he mused, and now him. Prime Minister. It had a ring, didn't it? Not bad for an Old Wykehamist who took a ropey third in land economy and only avoided jail because they couldn't spell his name properly.

A cough made him turn. Leopold Raddle stood in the doorway, unctuously rubbing his hands. The dry rasping made Hieronymus wonder if he ever triggered an accidental conflagration.

'Prime Minister…'

Hieronymus shut his eyes and smiled. Yes, he was going to enjoy this.

'It is time.'

Time? Catchpole, his supercilious SPAD, had mentioned something, hadn't he? Raddle was the longest serving member of the Cabinet Office's permanent secretariat and, by reputation, the oldest civil servant, appointed before decimalisation and the decriminalisation of single sex golf clubs. How he survived was a mystery…

'Remind me, Raddle.'

Raddle turned. 'Oh, there's no need to pretend you know what this is about, Prime Minister. No one but me knows what I'm about to tell you.'

Hieronymus stood, hesitating somewhere between being intrigued and shit-scared, and finally followed the wrinkled old retainer. The old boy kept talking as he led the country's new leader through a sequence of increasingly ancient, thick and secure doors, locking each as they passed.

'Each PM takes this walk, sir. It's to explain why, in the words of that old saw "all political careers end in failure".'

'Make me welcome, why don't you?' mumbled Hieronymus.

Raddle stopped and did something with his lips that may have been a smile or, just possibly, the preparatory exercises undertaken by a carnivore as it assesses its prey. 'You are most welcome, Prime Minister. Here we are.'

The permanent sub-undersecretary carefully eased the chain that hung round his neck out of his tatty shirt. It held a small and shiny key, which he swung in front of Hieronymus. 'When Guy Fawkes entered Parliament supposedly to blow it up, he had, in fact, a different plan. Before he was caught, he and his co-conspirators buried a small vial deep in the foundations. In it, a sanctified curse had been placed. The import was to confine to purgatory on Earth those who purported to govern this country while a Protestant usurper sat on the throne.'

Hieronymus blinked and narrowed his eyes. 'This is a jape, right? Mucky Martindale put you up to this, didn't he? It smacks of that duplicitous little flibbertigibbet's twisted sense of fun.'

Raddle looked down and shook his head. 'You are the fourteenth premier to assume a joke, sir. Only three have taken this seriously.' He lifted his gaze and looked on Hieronymus with an infinite sadness. 'When Parliament burnt down in 1834, the curse was unfortunately released and, but for the swift actions of a group of dedicated exorcists and the secret assistance of the Pope in offering an ecucommunicantanation -'…'

'A what?'

'A papal suppressant. It held the curse at bay while they built this room. But, by the time they did so, some of the curse had taken hold. See…'

Raddle turned and opened the door, standing back to let the very reluctant prime minister past. He stared at the tableau that faced him through a glass screen. 'The room is a controlled environment with each corner housing a true relic of the Cross and the glass is frequently doused in holy water blessed by the Bishop of London. While those controls remain, the angel you see, which represents that papal anaesthetic, holds the dove of peace above the donkey and so controls the curse. Meanwhile, this country will continue its bumbling but largely successful course while only one person will suffer the consequences…'

Hieronymus nodded. Weird but harmless, he thought. The old boy needs pensioning off if this is his idea of a bit of fun. 'Right ho. I'd better get back. Red boxes to read, you know.'

'Before you go, sir, you'll need to rub the donkey's head. It's tradition and ensures the curse remains dormant apart from your role.'

'Seriously?'

But Raddle had already used the key to open a small panel next to the donkey that allowed a hand to be inserted. 'Sir?' Raddle stood back, his expression inscrutable.

'Oh bollocks,' Hieronymus muttered, 'if I have to…' He reached in and touched the donkey. As he did so he slumped to the floor.

*

Some sort of tentacle appeared from the shadows and dragged the inert body away. Moments later, an exact replica of Hieronymus Hampton stepped forward. Raddle smiled, a proper smile. He stood in front of the frankly bemused doppelgänger. 'The donkey represents all prime ministers. You come into office with these plans and projects and before you know it, you'll make a right bugger's muddle, won't you? But someone must pay…'

The man nodded. Something like dawning understanding was filling his features.

'So, what you won't do is interfere with these basements or do anything that might make you universally popular. You'll see to that, won't you?'

The new Hieronymus nodded enthusiastically.

'The sniggerers, of which you are one, get a term, at best. Those who take this seriously but don't believe in it, might be allowed two terms. Only those who at least try to believe get to win three elections on the trot. And they will forever be excoriated for their presumption, be it a poll tax obsession or a dusty war. All of you will be humiliated. Failure. And when you leave office, you'll get your original body back, though not your memory, to enjoy a much-loathed retirement. Meanwhile…'

They both turned and looked at the donkey, which looked back at them through the glass. There was something of a shaggy-haired blond Wykehamist about it.

Pettifore And The Duster Of Doom

Pettifore Ptarmigan entered adulthood on the 27th of February via a set of steps and a badly painted door. He knew he was finally a grown up because the crowd in the small poorly lit room – which oddly smelt of cardamom and his grandfather after his annual deforestation – merely made space for him to sit and then ignored him. Before this moment, the usual reception on his entering a strange room was either "what do you want, kid?" or "put the pizzas over there".

No, Pettifore was now an adult, he just knew it; after all, wasn't being treated with indifference by strangers and being able to drink tea without sugar, the two badges of his much-awaited and much-delayed maturation?

The reason why Pettifore had chanced into this throng was to hear Dr (self-styled) Robinia Bellibrace discuss her latest theories on the existence of a previously undiscovered race of two-dimensional beings she had dubbed the Flatians with a depressing lack of imagination. Flatians, so the good doctor posited, were able to avoid detection by turning sideways on being disturbed, thus rendering themselves virtually invisible to the unquestioning eyes of mankind. The crowd murmured its apparent approval at this explanation for the century's old ignorance of the Flatians' arrival and colonisation of a small and rather moist suburb of what later became Ruislip. Pettifore, who was still slightly stunned about his accession to the land of men, missed the start of the sparse applause and, in an effort to catch up, did what he wanted to avoid: he brought the room's attention to his presence by an overvigorous clapping.

Dr Bellibrace leant across the lectern and peered at him with a predatory glint in her eye. 'Yes, exactly. We need such obvious enthusiasm if we are to obtain compelling evidence of the Flatians' existence. Let's follow this young man's lead.'

Pettifore concentrated on the "man" rather than the "young" and nodded hard.

'Who will join me,' Robinia intoned, 'in setting a trap for a Flatian?'

Pettifore, new and naive as he was, shot his hand in the air, sure that he would be one in a sea of limbs. It took him several moments to realise he was alone and the crowd about him had begun to ease away from his seat. An elderly man, sporting MacDonald spats and an octagonal squint, sighed. 'Brave, but really?'

Robinia could barely contain her excitement. She jabbed her finger at various parts of the crowd. 'You will see. We will have our proof.'

When Pettifore and Robinia arrived at 27 The Pleasants, Pettifore's home, Mrs Ptarmigan answered the door, apparently quite flustered. She had her hair held in a knotted scarf and wore rubber gloves that came up to her armpits. 'I'm trying to unblock your grandfather, dear. He's superannuated his grublings again. You make yourselves comfy in the sitting room while I make tea.'

While Pettifore sat nervously on a novelty canon, Robinia prowled the small room. Finally, she announced, 'This place is perfect. I'll set up a trap.'

Before Pettifore had a chance to conjugate Amo, his default calming chant, Robinia had triangulated the Chesterfield and armoured her strobing kaleidoscope. As Pettifore watched, entranced, gradually the reflection of a vibrant scene of shimmering ephemeral figures in dazzling primary colours appeared on the glass of the French doors. A beautiful woman with hair to spare offered a bowl of succour to an unseen underling.

Pettifore gasped as Robinia smiled. 'With the two of us,' she said, 'we can capture this image and consign the cynics and naysayers to the pit of humiliation. Come, boy, and hold the trap.'

To Pettifore, the trap appeared to be a plastic sleeve, but he was too polite and, in truth, a bit narked at being called a boy to much care.

He stepped forward and together with Robinia, he leant towards the glass.

*

'Right ho, who takes milk?' Mrs Ptarmigan bustled in and stopped. She took in the unlikely scene of two people apparently rapt, gazing at one pane of glass. She came to a hasty conclusion, pulled a duster from the pocket of her pinafore and pushed past Pettifore. 'I'm so sorry,' she apologised to a startled Robinia, 'but grandfather does tend to leave residues in the most unexpected places.'

With a swift and decisive rub, she decimated the small colony of Flatians and set back intergalactic anthropology several minutes. 'Tea?'

Robinia nodded, her energy levels clearly dropping.

'And maybe a chocolate Hobnob. You look like you need a sugar boost.' Mrs Ptarmigan held out the plate.

Corona

'Well, I'll be blowed.'

Janice Scrutt stuck her head through the loft hatch. 'What is it, Roger?'

Roger Scrutt pulled a dusty black leather box out from behind the water tank. 'Dad's old typewriter. I thought Mum said she'd got rid of it.'

Janice climbed down the ladder, muttering just loud enough for Roger to hear, 'When did she ever get rid of something?'

Roger's grinning face appeared through the hole. 'Hey, that's my mother you're accusing of being an incorrigible hoarder.' He reached down, the old case hanging from his fingers. 'Here you go.'

As she reached up, dust and debris fell on her face. 'Geez.'

He laughed. 'There's probably some of Dad in that dust.'

Wiping her tongue on her sleeve, she felt close to throwing up. 'Oh great. I've ingested your dad.' She dropped the case by her feet. 'You will get rid of this, won't you?'

'Course.' His voice already sounded distant and, to her ears, insincere.

When, half an hour later, it was still where she'd left it, Janice sighed and carried it to the heap of rubbish that was growing exponentially.

Four hours later, Roger locked the front door to his mother's house and climbed into the driver's seat. He leant across to kiss his wife. 'Thanks for helping.' He licked his lips. 'You even taste of Dad.'

'Stop it. I'll need counselling.' Janice groaned as she took in her grime-encrusted jeans and hands. 'Wine. I need wine.' She settled back into her seat for a snooze. She'd be pleased when the dirty old mausoleum was empty and sold. Whatever Roger said, not all his memories were ones to cherish.

Janice woke with a start, momentarily disorientated. They were home. She climbed out and stretched. Roger had his head buried in the boot.

'Do you want to make us a drink while I empty this lot?'

'Oh no.' Playfully, she elbowed him out of the way. 'I'll empty the car, thank you. I know you. You'll have tried to sneak something past me.'

He held up his hands in mock surrender. 'Not guilty, your honour!' He grinned and headed for the house.

She tugged the cardboard box of his old books to her; even her ruthless decluttering instincts hadn't been sufficient to deny him these. As she pulled, something fell over. Peering behind the box, she mouthed, 'You sod, Roger Scrutt,' and dropped the box onto the drive. The old typewriter case lay on its side. Oh no, not on your nelly. Leaving the books, she hefted the typewriter to the rubbish bin and dropped it inside. Grinning, she thought, Roger Scrutt, you will pay for that deception.

*

Monday mornings were always chaotic. While Roger knotted his tie with one hand and buttered toast with the other, Janice read her overnight mails as she applied lipstick.

'Can you put out the bins? I forgot last night.'

She scowled at him and then stuck out a tongue. 'If you feed Mandela. Oh, and refresh his water.'

Twenty minutes later, she headed outside, swinging her car keys around a finger. She nearly forgot the bins; spinning on her heels, she hauled them to the road. Why the bloody bin men couldn't walk the few yards to fetch them she would never understand.

She had half-turned back to the car when a thought occurred to her. She opened the lid and peered inside. Oh, you tricky man. The old typewriter had gone. Right. She headed back inside and for the garage. If she knew her husband, she knew where she'd find it.

Sure enough, it sat on the bench. He hadn't even tried to hide it. The arrogance. Tonight, she would give him so much grief. She smiled to herself. And then they could make up... She picked up the case and hefted it out to the bin.

*

Two days later, Roger sat in his ground floor office at home, studying the weeds in the garden. His father never allowed a weed to show its face; it was like a personal insult. He shut his eyes and saw his father, the back of his neck reddened from the sun and effort as he cursed the weeds out of the beds. Funny, Roger thought, Dad spent hours in that garden and never expressed any joy at his achievements, never once sat and enjoyed it. He didn't garden, Roger realised; he wrestled plants. WWF: William Wrestling Foliage.

Roger sighed. Normally, working at home was a pleasure, but today all he had were memories. He should begin that family history he had promised himself. Unable to settle, he headed for the kitchen and coffee.

The door to the garage was open. Had it been open earlier? Maybe, but still, he'd better check. A cursory glance showed doors and windows all shut; he turned to leave when he spotted it: the old typewriter case, all clean. Janice, you sneaky little minx, he thought. She'd given him grief about it and here it was. Carefully, almost reverently, he eased back the lid. She'd cleaned the old Corona and replaced the ribbon. A crisp new sheet sat in the roller, "Write Me" neatly typed in the centre. Ha, so she wanted him to write that history, too. Who was he to argue?

Lifting the case, he hurried back to his desk. He'd start it, surprise her with it. His work could wait.

He opened the case and took out the typewriter to put on the desk. The foot caught on the base and lifted it. Intrigued, Roger picked at the corner until it came loose. There were some closely typed sheets hidden beneath, which he pulled out. The heading made him start – *this is for you, Roger* - and his hands shook slightly as he read.

*

Roger was so engrossed he didn't notice the shadow, nor hear the slight click. When the hand touched his shoulder and he looked round, he couldn't comprehend what he saw. He clutched at his chest, the pain almost unbearable.

*

Six months later

Janice pulled open the front door, noticing the flaking paint as if for the first time. It grated that she was still unable to get a grip on things.

'Mrs Scrutt? Detective Inspector Thorne. I met you when…'

'When Roger died. Yes, I remember.' She thought he was a sergeant, but things had been awfully confused. Janice fought back a shudder of memory. This man had been the one who confirmed Roger was dead. What an awful job. She had hated him then, in that moment. Now, with a little distance, she felt a surge of compassion.

The policeman nodded, his gingery quiff bouncing with each movement. She remembered that quiff, thinking it made him look younger than he probably was. 'It's not about that. Well, not directly.'

How would she describe that expression? Cryptic? Confused? Certainly awkward. 'Would you like to come in?' She didn't wait on his response, before turning on her heels and heading towards the back and the kitchen. He could close the door. She needed a moment to compose herself. It might have been a few months, but time hadn't eased much of the horror: finding her husband at his desk, eyes stretched impossibly wide as the terror of what was happening hit him and that strange grey streak that appeared in his hair.

The autopsy said it was heart failure. He had a genetic weakness. It might have happened at any time. What no one had ever been able to explain, certainly not to her satisfaction, was his expression. It was real terror. If the death was as sudden as they said, why that look? And how was there time for that grey to appear in his hair? She was sure they didn't believe her when she explained it wasn't there before. She saw it in their expressions, in the if-you-say-so-madam scepticism, at least at the start. The whispers she may or may not have been meant to hear. Then the evidence emerged that it was dyed, but no hair colour products were found that might have been used. Not that that seemed to matter much, either. Maybe he'd had it done at work, they said.

This one, though, this Detective Thorne, she recalled as she waited for him to join her, he'd not been so sneering. Thorne – what was his first name? Peter? He seemed surprised when she showed him a photo of Roger's father in the year before he died. With the exact same streak.

She busied herself with a kettle, while she listened to him settle onto a stool. 'Tea or coffee?'

'Coffee, thanks. Can I ask how you've been?'

She put down a cup and some milk and sugar while she prepared a cafetière. 'Have I moved on, do you mean? Hardly. He's buried, but you know that I imagine. I've managed to sort out most things. So, me? Good and bad. Up and down. Grief is an indifferent and inconsistent companion.' She splashed hot water into the jug. 'Strong or weak?'

'Strong would be great. Yes, I can imagine.' He smiled and sipped. 'I'm sorry if I sounded rather cryptic earlier.'

Yes, cryptic would describe him, she thought. Same as before, holding things back. She nodded for him to carry on and sat opposite him.

'It's about your husband's family home.'

'Pottinger Cottage? We... I sold that a couple of months ago. When the probate came through.'

'To Patricia and Colin Normanby?'

'That's right.'

'I wondered how much you knew about the cottage.'

Janice stared at her coffee, a black granule floating in a random pattern on the surface. 'I never lived there. His parents inherited from his grandfather, his paternal grandfather. I think it may have been in the family for about fifty years?'

'And it was part of a farm?'

'Originally, yes. His grandfather ran Yallop Farm until he became too ill to carry on. Roger's father took it over. My impression was he didn't want to but felt some compulsion. He sold off the farm and land but kept the cottage. His parents had preferred living in the cottage, so I suppose it was a sentimental decision, but the place gave me the creeps.'

'Really? How so?'

'Oh, I don't know. It was cold for a start. I always shivered when we arrived, however hot it was outside. And there were the usual range of creaks and moans that go with old buildings that could give you – me anyway – the willies. And there was this odd smell, outside the back door. Sort of drainy even though the drains were on the other side of the building.'

The policeman checked his notes. 'It was a smell that led to us being involved.'

Janice raised an eyebrow but let him continue.

'His mother stayed there until she died?'

'Yes. Stupid really. We told her she should leave, come and live with us, but she had this misplaced loyalty to her husband, my father-in-law, Gerald. She died there. We'd been clearing the place out, ready to sell it a couple of days before… before Roger died.'

'I remember. When the place was part of a farm, did they keep pigs?'

Janice looked up sharply. 'Why?'

'Did the pigs live near the cottage?'

'I'm sorry, I don't know.' She stopped to swallow and take a sip of coffee. Another shudder, like the first one when he arrived, ran down her spine and she fought to keep her voice even. 'From memory, the only animals Gerald kept by the time Roger and I started going out were some goats. He had this thing about his garden and used goats to keep the grass on the left side shorn.'

'The garden is strange, isn't it?'

'I never understood why they didn't dig it up or lay it to grass. There was this patch outside the dining room where the only thing that ever grew were brambles, you know, blackberries, but the fruit was disgusting, really bitter.'

Another knowing nod. 'You remember nothing about when they stopped keeping the pigs and why? What happened to the herd?'

'No, I don't think it was ever mentioned.'

He sighed.

'What's this about?'

The inspector took a moment and then pulled out a plastic evidence pouch. Inside was a brown envelope and a sheet of A4 paper. Janice stared at it, unable to move.

'The Normanbys were disturbed by a foul smell when they started to landscape the garden. They wondered if there may be an old cesspit somewhere. They did indeed find a pit. At first it looked like it just contained animal bones.'

Janice's voice was barely a whisper. 'Pigs?'

He nodded. 'It was when they started pulling them out, they found this envelope.' He tapped the plastic evidence pouch. 'Intriguing, isn't it?'

Janice had already seen the addressee on the envelope. Her name, including, as if to make sure there was no confusion, her maiden name. But that wasn't the main thing that stopped her breath. It was the A4 sheet next to the envelope inside the plastic evidence pouch. Every spare inch comprised one word. "Help".

She looked at the inspector. Yes, his first name was Peter, she was sure. His smile seemed to offer sympathy for what he was doing. 'This must come as a tremendous shock, Mrs Scrutt. Given the decomposition of the animals, it's decades since that pit was dug and filled in.'

'The letter was buried a long time ago?'

'That's the odd thing. We are doing some tests, but it looks like the paper is the sort that was developed from computer printers, so unlikely to be more than five or six years old.'

'That's… how can it be there?'

'We don't know. We'd like to understand that ourselves. There are a few theories.'

'Yes?' Janice began to feel calmer. 'How strange. Though why are the police involved? Dead pigs aren't criminal, are they?'

'No. Ordinarily, we wouldn't have anything to do with this. It was the fact there were also human remains in the pit that has us interested.'

'Human remains?' The calmness began to evaporate.

He finished his coffee. 'Oh yes, this is one strange hole. Pigs, a human hand, a letter addressed to you and, perhaps most bizarrely, an old typewriter. A Corona.'

Janice's voice wobbled. 'A typewriter?'

'Yes, we ran a check for fingerprints. If you recall, we took yours for elimination purposes when we investigated your husband's death. Yours are on it. I don't suppose you can explain that?'

Janice thought she'd faint; excusing herself, she hurried to the bathroom where she splashed cold water on her face and sat on the edge of the bath to compose herself. This didn't feel real.

*

Inspector Thorne hadn't moved when Janice returned.

She sat, breathing hard. He'd pretty much accused her of being involved in the mysterious burial of human remains, so her silence wasn't a surprise.

He was about to ask if she needed more time when she said, 'Just a minute,' and, without another word, she disappeared once again into the hallway. Briefly, he wondered if she was about to do a runner. Then the possibility she was hunting out a weapon came to him.

He relaxed slightly when he heard her steps as she went upstairs. Whatever she was after didn't take her long to find as she was back inside five minutes. She placed a folder on the table between them as she sat, facing him, her hand on top. 'After Roger died, it took a while, but eventually I cleared out his clothes. The jacket he had worn that last day was on a chair in here. I remember not being able to move it for several days. It was…' he watched as she struggled with her emotions, 'I felt that if I left it, he might come back for it. I hung it in the hall cupboard, so it was weeks before I checked the pockets. I found a sheet of paper in the inside pocket.' She opened the folder and pulled it out. 'I couldn't make head nor tail of it.'

Peter Thorne turned it to face him, with the minimum contact with his finger, not wanting to compromise any forensic evidence. At the top, a date was typed, the day Roger had died, and underneath, also typed, was the same word, over and over.

Help

'It looks the same as that sheet.' She tapped the plastic pouch. 'I'm no expert, but it looks like the same typewriter was used, if that broken "p" is anything to go by.'

He checked she was happy for him to take the sheet. He pulled on some nitrile gloves before slipping it inside another evidence pouch. He studied it alongside the sheet he'd brought. They could be the same.

Janice broke the tense silence. 'Do you think it might be that Corona? The one in the pit?'

He shrugged. 'We can get it tested.'

She rubbed her face. 'We were clearing the cottage, as it had gone on the market. Roger focused on the attic. He found his dad's old typewriter, stuck behind the water tank. It was a Corona. Obviously it can't be the same as the one in the pit.'

She looked at the inspector for confirmation, but he kept a neutral expression.

'Roger said he was happy to throw it out, but he tried to keep it. I suppose… There couldn't be two typewriters with the same defect?

Could there? I mean, if the one he found did have that damaged "p" maybe he typed the note I found in his jacket.'

'Or,' Thorne pinched the bridge of his nose, 'he found the note when you were doing the clear out and he forgot to tell you?'

They both lapsed into silence. She said, 'He can't have found the note, though. Not with the date.'

'Maybe he added that. I know, why would he?' This time the inspector shrugged. He turned the evidence pouches over, hoping to find something that might explain this mystery. 'It looks like he typed this. Given the date and it's in his jacket. But probably not on the typewriter in the pit. And how do we explain the similarity between the notes?'

Her shrug suggested indifference. 'I kept the note because of the date. I… I could never believe he just died, you see. You remember that grey streak? I… felt there might be another explanation.'

'Such as?'

'I don't know. Nothing makes any sense. But if he typed it, it was the last thing he did. Or it felt that way. What was he trying to say?'

'I'd be very grateful if you'd tell me what you've been thinking, however bizarre. You never know.'

He waited for her to react. Finally, she took a large breath and opened the folder from which she'd extracted the original sheet. He could see other sheets. 'I nearly threw it away, when I first saw it. That *help,* it made me sick. But then I found these. At his mother's. I had to finish the clear out before a buyer came in.' She went to lift the sheets, but he stopped her, pulling on more gloves. She didn't try and stop him as he looked at each one.

'They were tucked in books on his mother's bookcase. The first fell out when I started emptying the shelves. Then a second. After that I shook every book.' She made as if to fan them out, even though he held them. 'Some are covered in just one word, repeated, like the one you found; some have a single word. *Help, pigs, shame.*' She paused, until he looked up at her. 'And then there's the name: Colin.'

'Colin?'

'One of Roger's brothers is called Colin. Roger was the youngest of three; his older brothers were twins. I think they were, maybe five years older. They disappeared when Roger was fifteen or sixteen. The other twin brother was called Christopher.'

'Did you know him, then?' He checked his notes. 'You went to school together, didn't you?'

'I moved to the same school as him in the sixth form, shortly after they left. I knew of Roger, but we didn't get together until after university.'

Thorne turned over the pages of his notes. 'I don't have anything about the brothers' disappearance. Was it reported, do you know?'

'I think, at the time, they'd had a falling out with their father and left to work in London. That's what Roger said. They were adults - twenty-one, I think, and he didn't want to talk about it because it upset his parents. And by the time his father died they'd been gone so long. He, Roger, tried to find them, but he gave up when his mother found out. Her view was they'd have got back in touch if they'd wanted to and should be left alone.' She looked wistful. 'After she died, he said he'd look for them, but he didn't pursue it. If he'd lived, he might have gone looking again, I suppose. It played on his mind I think.'

'How so?'

'There was the odd comment when we were packing up old family photos. A sense of regret that he'd not done more.'

'And back when they first disappeared, you don't think they were reported missing at that time?'

'I don't really know. Sorry.'

The policeman wrote some more notes. 'Do you happen to have anything of your late husband's – a hairbrush or similar?'

'Why?'

'The bones we found. The hand. If we can find his DNA, we may be able to find enough to establish if there is a familial link.'

'You think it might be Colin?'

'Or Christopher. Or both?'

'Both? You only mentioned a hand?'

'We're re-examining the site. It's possible the pigs...' He looked at the papers in front of him. 'They say pigs.'

She shuddered. 'I read somewhere about pigs being used to dispose of a body. Do you...?'

'I really can't speculate.' He studied her reaction. He might not be speculating, but he was sure she was. He waited again, until finally he judged she had absorbed the information. 'Can you confirm that the Corona, the one you say was your father-in-law's, would probably have your fingerprints on it?'

She nodded.

'And the last time you saw it?'

She looked pale and shook her head. 'I'm not sure. I think it was the day he died. The bin men were collecting that morning and as I said he was messing about, trying to keep it when we'd agreed to throw it out. I'm sure they must have taken it.'

'And between him finding it and it being taken, did you type anything? Can you remember touching any keys?''

She met his gaze, before answering, a quizzical expression on her face, 'Not especially. I didn't try and type anything, but it's possible I touched one or two when I picked it up.'

'And can you think of any other old Corona typewriter you may have touched?'

She pulled a face. 'No, I never typed before the advent of computer keyboards. I don't think...' She petered out, looking confused.

He nodded. This was going to give him a migraine, he just knew it. 'It's probably nothing, but please give it some thought. See what comes to mind.' His phone buzzed and he excused himself to take a call. He returned to say they would have to continue another time.

He was pleased to have a break, in truth, as the whole thing made no sense and he had more urgent matters calling for his attention.

*

As requested, Janice racked her brains to try and think of any sort of coherent explanation for these odd events, especially the typewriter in the pit in the garden. Nothing made sense and she refused to believe in the supernatural, even if her mind kept insisting that was the only explanation. She didn't see or hear from him for a few days; a constable came to take a DNA swab, but that was the only contact. She passed the young woman a box of cufflinks and other bits she'd kept as mementoes, in the hope they'd find some DNA of Roger's to use.

She was scraping at the flaking paint on the front door when a cough made her look up. It was Thorne, holding up a brown paper bag.

'Croissant?'

'Bribery?' She tried a smile; in truth, she appreciated the gesture, even if part of her felt sure she was a suspect.

When they had settled in the kitchen, Peter Thorne opened a briefcase and extracted a notebook. 'Those items of jewellery were very useful. We ran various DNA checks and there is a familial link between your husband and the hand, most likely a sibling.'

Janice screwed up her face. 'I assumed it must be. Only one though? You wondered if there might be evidence of both, didn't you?'

'I'm coming to that. This may be a shock, but there was also a match, albeit a different one, with you.'

'ME?!' She couldn't help squeaking in shock and surprise.

'You and your husband were half siblings. It seems most likely that your father and his were the same.' Thorne waited, knowing this would take some getting used to. 'I take it this is news to you?'

'News? Oh yes, you'd better believe that. Did Rog… No, you can't know that. He can't have known, can he? What about his mother? And his bloody father let us marry. How could he?' Her anger was morphing into tears. She stared at the anxious to please policeman, looking as if he really would prefer to be somewhere else.

He sipped his coffee, apparently waiting for Janice to regain some composure. 'We can continue later, if you like?'

She sat very still for a moment. 'Roger said he couldn't have children. Some genetic issue like Huntingdon's or something. I never pressed; I'd never really been that interested in children, if I'm being honest. Was that his way of making sure we didn't…? Oh God.' She covered her face and sobbed again. Finally, she tore off some kitchen roll, blew her nose and held the policeman's gaze. 'Was there more?'

'The remains are from one adult male. We believe from teeth marks on the bones that he was probably eaten by a pig, post-mortem. But the hand was left for some reason. I really came to talk about the typewriter. A full analysis has been done and it looks like your fingerprints were…' he seemed to struggle to explain. 'It's as if you wanted to leave them.'

'Sorry?' He wasn't making sense.

He spread his fingers in a parody of typing. 'There are prints on the middle line of keys. Imagine sitting in front of the typewriter and spreading your hands so your forefingers lined up next to each other in the middle, one on the "g" and the other on the "h". Then spread each hand out so the left set touches the "f", the "d" and the "s" and the right touch.'

'Margate!' She felt her eyes widen in surprise.

'Sorry?'

She stared at her hands for a moment. 'When you asked if I'd ever touched a Corona, I knew there was something niggling at me. It was…' She frowned and shook it away. 'I can't say exactly. This man asked me to sit at an old typewriter so he could take pictures of my hands on the keys. He got me to press them down.' She shook her head. 'I'd forgotten all about it until just then.' She pulled a face. 'It was so weird, that's why I remember it. We were at this event – Roger had been invited to it by some client, I think, to give a talk. I was waiting for him when this man approached and said he'd seen my hands, thought they were perfect for his purpose and did I mind if he photographed them.'

'And you let him? Did he say who he was?'

She paused a moment. 'It was a book event and I'm pretty sure he said he was a publisher or an agent, and they were looking for a pair of woman's hands with bright nail polish.' She waggled her fingers, revealing her unpainted nails. 'I used to love vibrant colours. He wanted them for a book cover.' She paused a beat. 'A murder mystery.'

Janice squirmed under the policeman's steely gaze. It was as if he was hunting for any sign she was making this up. But she felt oddly confident. This may explain the typewriter in the pit. If they could find the man and… Her heart sank. How likely was that?

'You're saying the typewriter in the pit in your in-law's garden might have been planted by someone who went out of their way to obtain your fingerprints on the keys? And this was, what? Some time before your husband died?'

She dropped her gaze and squeezed her eyes shut. 'It sounds ridiculous.'

'It's lacking a certain credibility on its own.' He pulled out some more sheets. They were blow ups of the pages Janice had found. 'Only your prints are on these pages. Not your mother-in-law's, not your husband's. Which might suggest you planted them. What is intriguing is the damaged "p". It's not the same as the letter we found in the pit. Our experts think it most likely someone has tried to mimic the damage to the original. It's close, but there are some tell-tale signs of tampering.'

'What does that mean?'

Thorne shrugged. 'A mystery or, in our line of work, a mess.' He proffered a smile, which wasn't returned. 'You said your husband had tried to find his siblings after his father died.'

'Yes, but he stopped when his mother asked him to.'

'And your in-laws didn't want their disappearance mentioned to us when they left?'

'That's what he said.' She paused. 'I've been thinking back about that. Roger went to some sort of detective agency, at one point.'

'Was this when his mother made him stop?'

'No, more recently. He had these old family photos and said how he should have tried to get back in contact. He regretted not doing more earlier.'

Thorne nodded.

'That was because of his parents. He was torn. Eventually he decided to try.'

'This was after your mother died?'

'He did but I have a memory of him saying he'd tried before and this time he'd get it right. He was always so easily upset that I always left him to say what he wanted to. I never pressed him.'

'He'd have told you, wouldn't he? If he tried?'

She hesitated. 'Not necessarily. As I say, he was touchy about that whole matter. And... things hadn't been great between us for a while. It's possible it happened when we were... when we were separated.' Though, in truth, she knew she couldn't be sure what had gone on.

'Did he say much about them? His brothers?'

She rubbed her face. 'Not really. He and his mother had a strained relationship, Inspector...'

'Please, Peter.'

She nodded, though it might have been an automatic reaction. 'She pulled him in so many directions. I think he wanted to find them, but he knew it would cause real problems. They were both very stubborn.'

'Did he mention the name of the agency he used?'

'I don't but... hang on.' She stood and pulled open a kitchen drawer, lifting out three battered address books. She chose one that was leather bound. 'Roger's business addresses.' She flicked through the pages and turned the book to face him. Under *investigation agency* there were two names and phone numbers. 'I'd guess one of these.' She shut her eyes tight. 'I went through this when he died, because, in truth, Inspector, my husband was secretive and I wondered if there was… I was sure there were things I didn't know. I wondered about these, but I've never tried to speak to them.'

'Secretive?'

'Money, mostly.'

The pages Janice had exposed showed a neat right-sloping handwriting. On the left side, as well as the two names and numbers she'd mentioned, there was a third that had been obliterated by a thick felt tip.

Thorne reached out and took it, holding it up to the light. 'We might be able to do something with this. Can I keep it?'

She nodded.

'One final thing for now. Did your husband have a laptop and mobile, which you still have?'

'His laptop has been reused. I don't have his phone.'

'Oh?'

'This area is rather prone to burglaries. We had a spate around here. Our nearly neighbours were done three times in as many months. I had two unwelcome visits. The second, just after he died, was when his phone went alongside some money, jewellery and cash.'

'And the first?'

'The car keys.'

'Joy riders?'

'They never took it. Roger said he'd get the locks changed, but when we found out how much it would cost, we decided to take our chances. The crooks never bothered. Is this relevant?'

'I don't suppose so. But I'm naturally curious.' The inspector scribbled some notes.

Janice watched him. He had a cute dimple when he was concentrating. When she looked up from his chin into his eyes, she saw that he was grinning at her and felt herself blush. To cover her confusion, she said, 'Do you think this may have something to do with the missing twin?'

'We think it's probably Colin who's dead. The one mentioned in the note.'

'Why do you think that? Beyond the fact Colin's name was on the typed page?'

'That was the other DNA match, with one Christopher Scrutt.'

'He's alive?'

'He was five years ago. It seems he was asked to give DNA for elimination purposes – there was a nasty sexual assault in a club where he was present. It wasn't him and the sample should have been destroyed, but…' he spread his hands in an apologetic gesture. 'Seems we slipped up and kept it.'

Janice studied his face. He smiled and she found herself smiling back. Maybe there would be an explanation. 'You think he's involved in some way?'

'I have no idea, but there are too many odd inconsistencies for us to ignore his possible involvement. Do you have the laptop?'

'I gave it to my brother. He runs a charity for the homeless and they need them for their clients. I'm afraid the hard drive has been wiped.'

'Can I have his details, to see if we can retrieve anything? If the budget allows, we might ask a boffin to see if they can get something.'

'What sort of something?'

'Any contacts your husband may have had with the investigation agency. And whether he was in contact with his brother.'

'You think that's possible?'

'Anything seems possible in this case.'

'What next?'

'More tests, more background digging. We may need to exhume your husband, I'm afraid.'

'Really? Why?' Her blood chilled, the smile long gone.

He swallowed. 'You remember that grey streak, in his hair?'

'I'll never forget it. It appeared out of nowhere. You people didn't believe me when I said it must have been dyed.'

'I've checked the details. It was dyed. Bleached anyway.'

'I said to someone that I didn't understand as there was nothing in the house he could have used. You… your colleagues didn't believe me.'

'Yes, as it wasn't thought to be suspicious…'

Her head spun. She tried to blink her way through the fug that surrounded her brain. 'You think it's suspicious now?'

He offered her no explanation. 'You'll appreciate all these anomalies make us curious in ways we weren't at the time. I had better go. If you think of anything at all, please call.'

'Of course.' She hesitated. 'Am I a suspect?'

'Suspect?'

'You know. Now you suspect Roger's death to be…' She couldn't say it.

He didn't help her. 'I'll be in touch.'

*

For the next few days, Janice Scrutt had trouble sleeping. The idea that her marriage was – what? Illegal? Certainly immoral was horrendous. Thinking of what her own mother would say of it, with her pinched Baptist beliefs and small village certainties, she broke out in a cold sweat. She'd been adamant her father had died before she was born, when he was working abroad. Why hadn't she questioned that? Had she been adopted? Could a single mother adopt? If only she'd asked more questions than just letting things slide. She knew why, of course: the fear that her mother had had her outside of wedlock and how she couldn't be the one to reveal that shame.

She tried to remember what she'd done with her birth certificate. Had she ever had it? She must have needed it for a passport. She could get a copy. That would tell her who her father was. That might give her something to do, though the whole thing made her sick. No, she'd leave that and focus on where this mystery started. With Roger and his brothers.

And then there were all those loose ends and the sense that the policeman was only telling her a limited version of all he knew. And behind all these circulating worries sat Roger's mysterious brother, Christopher. Had he really been alive all along?

She tried to piece everything together, not that it made much sense. It was easiest to write it down. Roger had lost two brothers, Colin and Christopher. It turned out one was dead and had been buried, or what was left of him, with the pig that had eaten him, in the back garden of her in-law's house. She tried to imagine what was now happening to that house and garden. Probably being pulled apart. The other brother was alive and had been involved, maybe innocently, five years ago in something. Was that when Roger had tried to find his brothers? There was no reason to link the events. Did he know of his brother's death? Her father-in-law's fixation with that garden might suggest he knew, but that didn't mean Roger knew, too. Or was there some link to the fact she and Roger shared a parent? God, that made her sick. Had he found out? Did he know?

And then there was the typewriter in the same pit, as well as the notes both in the pit and spread around her in-laws' house and hers. Why had someone attempted to make it look like they were typed on the same machine? And Roger's death. Was that innocent, albeit tragic? Or was it suspicious? She thought about the hair streak. It suggested some link back to his father. A thought occurred to her. There was no dye in the house after he died. She remembered those whispers from the police. She'd been determined to show she wasn't going mad. She'd searched everywhere. No, someone had to have visited that day and... and... She swallowed and wanted to scream. He'd been murdered. That's what the policeman wanted her to understand. They did tests that showed his heart failed. They probably didn't go looking for any chemical catalyst.

If it was her half-brother, how had he done it and why?

The next few days were easily the most appalling since Roger's death, possibly worse after the police decided on a public appeal to try and find Christopher Scrutt. Nothing happened and she felt like she was in limbo.

*

Ten days after the discovery of the pit, Inspector Thorne appeared with another policeman. Janice was taken to the police station and arrested in connection with the mysterious death of Colin Scrutt and warned they were also looking into the death of her husband, for whom they had sought an exhumation order.

She was appointed a solicitor, who appeared to be a rather flamboyant woman, with rainbow ribbons in her dreadlocks and a way of talking that, to Janice, suggested she was fighting boredom. If Janice had had the energy, she would have sacked Naomi Azruha and asked for someone else. They exchanged some perfunctory details.

The second time Janice met Naomi, the woman was wearing a dull green suit and appeared to be more engaged. She was tall and stooped, and this time spoke with a soothing dispassionate voice. 'I've been through everything and they don't have enough to charge you. Arresting you is police procedure. They won't oppose bail at this time.'

'Why would they think I'm guilty of anything?'

'It runs something like this, so far as they are giving me the full picture. The forensics suggest the victim in the pit wasn't eaten by the pig he was buried with – the teeth marks suggest a different animal. With the oddities around the typewriter and the note, it's possible items were added later.'

'And they think I did that?'

'You had opportunity, they say. Your mother-in-law was almost reclusive. Maybe you had help from your husband. Maybe, to him, the shame of the marriage was such that he wanted any evidence hidden. You found your husband's body. You said you were out all day, but there isn't any alibi to that effect, so you could have gone home, killed him, dyed his hair and then called the police. You could also have distributed the pages around both houses and you could have said you were burgled, and destroyed the phone yourself.'

'What about Margate? The man who photographed me?'

'They checked with Roger's place of work at the time. They have no recollection of any work event. According to the HR department it shows Roger took a day off at the last minute, citing a family event.'

'If... if Roger was killed, they'll say it was me, won't they?'

'The original autopsy said heart failure, but if there is any trace of poison...' Naomi shrugged and let the implications hang.

'Why would I do this? Bury the typewriter and note?'

'If you knew about the other brother being alive, but doing all he could to hide, you could put together something that makes it look like he was framing you, you and your husband.'

'A bit far-fetched.'

'Very. Personally, I think Thorne believes you, but those higher up want something concrete for the press. They need to find the brother. Why don't you take it easy for a while and let them pursue their inquiries.'

Janice nodded at that, but already her mind was turning over. The only thing that made sense to her was Roger's brother being involved. What could possibly motivate him? That same evening, she poured herself a scotch and sat in Roger's favourite chair with a notepad. Where could she look for help?

She began scribbling.

1. *Private detective hired by Roger?*

2. *Christopher Scrutt still using own name?*

3. *Margate typewriter?*

The only thing she could think to do was go back to Margate, to the hotel where she'd gone with Roger, and see if that led anywhere.

*

Margate was drab. A mean wind blew in from the North Sea, spinning the offshore turbines but otherwise doing little good, or so it seemed to Janice. She hunched into her coat as she walked quickly from the station, past the Turner Gallery and towards the Old Town.

The hotel was still there, albeit it was part of a chain and called itself the Bay Hotel. That morning, Janice had printed off the artist's impression of Christopher from the public appeal using the only photo she'd found of him when he was twenty. She thought it unlikely Christopher would have been the one to ask her to pose – Roger would have recognised him and surely Roger couldn't be in on some conspiracy. But he might have had a colleague or someone he'd paid trick her, so he may have been in the hotel. It had been a few years before and the chances of anyone still being there were small, but…

Two hours later she left, downcast because her assumptions were right, but still she held a glimmer of hope. The woman on reception had wanted to know why Janice wanted to speak to long-serving staff members, so she'd explained about the trickery and the typewriter, even if she'd avoided her own suspected role in any unlawful killing. When Janice finished talking to a member of the kitchen staff and returned to the reception to thank the woman, she'd pushed forward a sheet of paper, a printed page off the internet.

'It may be nothing, but there's a specialist second-hand typewriter shop in the Old Town. If you had time, you might ask there.'

Thomas Typewriters was the sort of shop that modern high streets had pushed out. Dusty windows were cluttered with more machines than there was room to display properly, and it didn't seem welcoming. As Janice pushed open the door, a bell sounded somewhere deep in the back. She stood at an old scuffed wooden counter, admiring a rather beautiful typewriter that stood proudly on the shelf in front of her.

'Lovely, isn't it? Real pieces of workmanship, not like the plastic rubbish of today.' The speaker was a man in his sixties, Janice guessed, dressed in saggy non-descript brown cords and a beige asymmetric cardigan over an oddly vibrant pink polo shirt. If his words suggested "curmudgeon", the eyes twinkled mischievously. 'How can I help?'

Janice swallowed and pulled out two pictures. The first was the artist's view of Christopher, the second an old picture of her father-in-law sat at his ancient Corona. 'This might seem odd, but a few years ago I was tricked into sitting at a typewriter like this one. The self-same model.'

The old man held the picture of the typewriter towards the light. 'A Smith Corona 14/72, 23 inch.'

'I wondered if you might have sold one to this man about that time.' She pushed a picture of Christopher across the table.

The old man peered at it and turned on his heels. 'Twenty-seven pounds, no bartering.' He disappeared through a beaded curtain for a few moments before returning with the ledger.

He thumped it down and began hefting pages, going backwards, hunting something. 'The man was rather brusque. He knew what he wanted and wasn't interested in any other machine. That is quite rare, especially for a machine like this one.'

Janice was fascinated despite herself. 'Why?'

'It's pretty crap, frankly. They tried a different way of fixing the letters - the aim was to try and avoid the keys jamming if someone typed really fast and it didn't work very well. The extremes – Ps, Os, Qs and Ws – were all prone to damage.'

'And you sold one to this man?'

The old man looked up, a rueful smile on his thin lips. 'I love these machines – many is the time they've been called my babies – and I tend to recall each one. But the buyers and sellers not so much. I recall the buyer's manner more than his face. Ah, here we are. Yes, he paid the price I'd proposed – most try a little bartering.'

'He didn't leave any details, did he? A name, address?'

The man put a liver-spotted hand over the entry. 'Should I be telling you? You may be a stalker?'

She looked up and saw the twinkle again. 'It would be really helpful.'

He took a moment and then spun the ledger round. It said Christopher Parsons. No address but a long number. She pointed at it.

'Back then, I didn't have one of the card machines. If a customer wanted to pay by a card – and frankly I discouraged it – I used a swipe machine. Before I sent the carbon to receive my credit, I wrote down the card details.'

'Can I?' She rummaged for a pen and a notebook.

'Don't tell him I let you.'

Back outside she shook. Christopher was common enough but Parsons – his mother's maiden name. It had to be him. She knew she should phone Thorne, but instead she headed for a café and pulled out her MacBook, logging onto the café's Wi-Fi. Typing in his new name and Margate, she decided to check the electoral roll.

It didn't take long. There were three Christopher Parsons in the Margate area. One was Christopher Alan and one Christopher Thomas. Roger's brother's middle name was Thomas. The third was just Christopher. She wrote down the addresses and decided to pay a visit, starting with Christopher Thomas.

This address was opposite another café where she sat in the window and had a sandwich. She hunted for public profiles on Facebook and other social media. One Christopher Thomas Parsons appeared to live in Margate still and his picture counted him out: he was black. As she pondered this fact, a man strolled past the window. It was the same man she'd just seen online. She'd found Christopher Thomas.

Facebook wasn't much help. There were hundreds of Christopher or Chris Parsons and none of the others referenced Margate. Feeling like she should hand over her new knowledge to the police, she thought she'd have a quick look at the address she had for Christopher Parsons.

This turned out to be an entirely residential area on the road towards Broadstairs, a small bungalow with a neat front garden and a battered-looking Ford on the drive. She hesitated and checked the address. Yes, this was it.

She felt very exposed so, glancing to either side, she moved away from the windows. They looked shut up, like the occupants might be away.

'Hi, can I help?'

Janice jumped.

A woman had emerged from the neighbouring house and stood, drying her hands on a dishcloth. 'I saw you looking. No one's home.'

Janice moved towards the woman, beginning to dig in her bag for the picture while she stepped forward, too.

'Are you his sister?'

'I… sorry?' Janice felt wrong-footed. She realised that if this was Roger's brother, the it was also her half-brother. 'Do we look that similar?'

'My God, yes! Your eyes are his, especially with that frown.' She laughed a deep belly laugh. The woman held out a hand. 'Marjory Oldsmith. Chris mentioned a brother but not a sister.'

'Half-sister. We… we're estranged. I've been trying to track him down.'

'Family trait, then?'

'Is it? I'm not sure I…' She opened her arms in a gesture of confusion.

'Chris has spent a lot of time tracking down your family, he said. Maybe you know this?'

She shook her head.

'He's not here, I'm afraid. Upped and left a while ago, not that that's unusual.'

'Oh. Oh well.' Janice wasn't sure where to go with the conversation. The woman, Marjory, seemed happy to talk. 'Could I maybe ask you about Chris? As I said, I've been looking for him for so long and I know so little.'

For the first time Marjory looked unsure. 'I suppose. Come on, come in and have a coffee.' She half-turned and then looked back. 'Have you seen a recent picture?'

Janice's heart went to her mouth. 'No, I've no pictures.'

Marjory smiled. 'Come on, then.'

*

Janice stared at the diffident man facing the camera. It looked like it was taken in a back garden, maybe at a barbecue. He had hooded eyes that were so like hers, she touched one eyebrow instinctively. Now he sported that goatee, the intervening twenty years explaining the receding hairline. She focused on the eyes, before remembering his small round sunglasses had hidden them from her. It could be the same man as in the police reconstruction. Possibly.

'What happened? I mean, why were you separated? If you don't mind saying?'

'I'm his half-sister. I didn't know until very recently when there was a query – DNA – and it came out I was related to his brother who had died. That's when I found out about Christopher. He may not know his brother is dead so, well, I thought it was a good excuse to try and find him.' Was she speaking too fast? It was the truth, sort of.

'He knows his brother's dead. It… he's been in a strange place since he came back and told me.'

'Are you close?'

Marjory shook her head and then looked down at her hands, spinning a ring on her right hand. 'We had… well, at one point…' She laughed awkwardly. 'We were good for each other. He's a good listener.'

'What's he like?'

'Quiet. Intense. A bit lonely, I'd say. Very private. I didn't know much about his family, apart from his mother. He was close to her.'

'How long has he lived here?'

'In Margate? All his life, he said. His parents moved away and he came back after university and stayed. He works for the council, something to do with engineering. His mother seemed lovely.'

Janice tried hard to hide her surprise. 'You met her?'

'Why yes. She visited quite regularly. She'd come on a Tuesday, occasionally, and go home the next evening.'

Janice squeezed her eyes shut. Her mother-in-law had a "friend" in Canterbury who she visited every month or so. Only now, it turned out the "friend" was Christopher, or so it seemed. She fiddled with her phone and found a picture of her mother-in-law. She turned the screen to face Marjory. 'Is this his mother?'

Marjory nodded. 'And that's Roger, his brother.' Her finger hovered over the image of Janice's husband.

She forced herself to speak. 'Did… did Roger visit, too?'

Marjory nodded. 'I saw him a couple of times but only spoke to him the once. I'd been in hospital – a small procedure – and they released me early. I think it was the weekend and they must have figured they could better use the bed than have me filling it. I told them Chris would be able to keep an eye on me, so the ambulance men who brought me back knocked and he and Roger came over. He seemed very nice. Less like his brother, less serious. That was the only time we spoke…. Now, when was that? April? It must be six months ago, maybe a bit longer. I can check the dates if it's important. They were arguing.'

Janice turned to face the window, trying to imagine what prompted Roger to turn up and why he'd not said, why he'd talked about finding his brothers.

'Would you like more tea?'

'That…yes, thank you.'

Marjory disappeared towards the back of the house. She called after Janice, 'It's a shame you missed him. I expected him back last week, but I've not heard anything. It's a bit of pain, in truth.' She re-emerged and put the pot down. 'Colin is very demanding.'

Janice felt her shoulders go rigid. Colin was the dead twin. What did she mean?

Marjory didn't notice as she concentrated on pouring more tea. 'He's a rescue, from abroad, and if he doesn't get his feed on time, he's yowling like he's being tortured.'

Janice blinked at the teacup that was being handed to her. 'A cat?'

'His true love, I used to say. He dotes on that moggy. I'm cat-sitting, but I'm off tomorrow for a few days at my sister's.' She looked at her hands again. 'We've tickets to see a tribute act and, well, it'll be a bit of fun. If he's not back, I'm not sure what to do.' She laughed. 'Godfrey, on the other side, tried to feed Colin once and the cat went berserk. He ended up in A&E. Apart from Chris, he won't tolerate men.'

Janice swallowed and held her breath. 'I could…'

'Sorry?'

'I mean… what I mean is I'm in Margate for a few days and could pop in. If that would help. Kind of begin making up for lost time.'

Marjory's face contorted into several unspoken questions. 'I'm not sure. I mean, I've only just met you. And he's very private. Plus Colin might not take to you.'

'I understand if the idea makes you uncomfortable.'

'Well, you clearly know the family. You have that picture.'

'I've other pictures of Roger, too, if that helps?'

'No, really.' She tapped her fingers nervously on her lap. 'Tell you what. Come with me now, and we can feed his majesty and see if he'll tolerate you. If not, that answers it. If he does, then I'll call Chris's mobile and leave a message. If he's coming home or rings and says not, then fine, but if he remains incommunicado, well, let's do it.'

'If it helps, I'll check in with this neighbour. Godfrey? Just to let him know it's me.'

'Would you? That would make me more comfortable.'

'Of course. I just want to help. It's rather exciting at my age to find I have a new brother and to help him is the icing on the cake.' She was sure Marjory would see through the lie, but she was in too deep now to stop.

Thirty minutes later, Janice stood on the pavement, looking at Christopher's bungalow. She left her mobile number on the proffered notepad. She hesitated briefly when Marjory suggested giving Chris her number, but what else could she do?

The cat ignored her when Marjory led them into the spotless kitchen and, after, when they popped round, Godfrey nodded his understanding of the proposal. It just needed Marjory to call and set up the handover of the keys, assuming Christopher didn't return over the next twenty-four hours.

*

Sitting in the reception to the hotel, waiting to be shown to a room, she wondered if she was mad. She should call Inspector Thorne and tell him what she'd uncovered. But curiosity is a strong emotion.

A text message came in at 9pm, saying Marjory had heard nothing. The key and a note of instructions would be under her front door mat for the morning feed. Marjory finished by thanking Janice for saving her bacon.

*

By 8.30, Janice had checked in with Godfrey and collected the key and the promised note. The key was a simple Yale – not the most secure. As she walked down the path on her way to Christopher's back door, she opened the note. It was a neatly typed set of feeding and watering instructions. On the top Marjory had written:

Chris called back late last night. He said he was delighted you would be feeding Colin and was looking forward to meeting you just as soon as possible…

Janice nearly gave up then and there. If she hadn't already told Godfrey, who she sensed was watching her, she might have turned and run away. Instead, she took a deep breath and opened the door.

'Hello?'

Silence. Taking several breaths, she headed for the kitchen and eased open the door. The tins of food were in the high cupboard near the sink. She was just reaching up, when a sound like a door opening triggered a squeal.

She turned to see the cat flap swinging madly and Colin twisting in circles near his bowl as he waited for the food.

Concentrating on mundane tasks made it easier to relax a little. The cat was as good as gold and, to Janice, rather lovely. She sat on a barstool by the breakfast bar and watched the cat eat with dainty nibbles. She should go, call the police and leave it at that. They could do all the questioning they wanted, which was more than she could. Still, now she was here…

She re-entered the hall and wondered what to do. She wished she'd brought some latex gloves. She imagined the police doing a forensic sweep of the place and if her prints were everywhere… She returned to the kitchen to look under the sink. A pair of pink rubber gloves sat on top of some cleaning materials. Feeling slightly foolish, she put them on and went back to the hall. As she turned to go up the stairs, she noticed the cat had sneaked ahead of her and now stood at the top as if barring her way. She wondered if he might attack her, as he had apparently done to Godfrey, if she tried to push past him. She was being silly; she needed to be methodical, that's all.

Keep cool, she told herself. That made her turn back to the front door and slip on the chain. If Christopher did return, or anyone else come to that, she'd know soon enough.

Struggling with the gloves, she opened the first door on her right. A bedroom. The wardrobe had clothes and shoes but no interesting boxes. There was nothing under the bed or the mattress as far as she could judge. The second bedroom produced some boxes, but they were a mixture of old crockery, some paintings done by an amateur – Christopher? – and old clothes. The bathroom was even less interesting. She headed downstairs and checked the lounge. There was a photograph of his mother, amongst several of him and his father at a much younger age. The one of his mother was clearly on a visit, but that was all. Finally, after an hour, she stood in the kitchen again. The place lacked personality, apart from the photos, as well as anything that might explain a link to her and Roger.

A thought occurred. She peered into the garden. At the far end sat a small shed. The door was clearly padlocked. Remembering a keyboard in the hall, she retraced her steps and checked the keys. Sure enough, one said "shed". Smiling, she headed outside, careful to keep her head lower than the fence and hoping no one nearby was in a back bedroom and looking out.

Her hands shook as she unlocked the door and pulled it open. It was musty and crammed with garden paraphernalia, much more than she imagined he would need for the size of garden. Maybe he was very keen. She began to pull tools away from the walls and checked under sacks and in the drawers of an old desk that held string and labels and seeds of all kinds. Nothing. This was hopeless. She needed to lock up and call the inspector.

Pulling open the door, she stepped out into the sunshine and froze. Standing a few feet away, Christopher Scrutt or Parsons faced her, a small tight smile playing on his lips. 'My sister Janice? So kind of you to want to look after the garden as well as the cat.' He nodded at her hands. 'And some cleaning, too?'

Janice had a job holding herself together.

'Do I get a kiss? This is some reunion, don't you think?'

'I... how do you know I'm your sister?'

'Sister-in-law. I thought, with my brother, your husband, dead, the informality might be appropriate. I didn't mean to offend. Come. Let's have a cup of tea and you can tell me how you found me. Shall I take those gloves?'

'Why were you hiding?'

He looked pained. 'I imagined you might have known. No one said?'

'No.'

'All the more reason for tea and confessions. Please.' He stood back and indicted the back door.

Janice glanced around desperately, hoping to see an escape route. The back gate stood behind him, firmly shut and padlocked. She had no way of scaling the six-foot panels that surrounded the garden and screaming might lead to an extreme reaction. She took in a breath and headed for the house, wondering how easy it would be to get to her phone, currently sitting in the bottom of her bag on the work counter.

'Why don't you go and get settled in the sitting room and I'll come through with tea.'

She nodded, keen to get away from him. She picked up her bag and moved towards the hall. As soon as the kitchen door shut behind her, she made for the front door. The chain was on, but it would be easy to unlatch. She would be outside and on the street in moments, where she could call Thorne. She felt a weight lift as she took hold of the chain and lifted it free. She pulled the door latch hard.

Nothing. She yanked harder, now desperate. The door refused to move. The mortice lock had been applied and, without a key, she wasn't going anywhere.

The kitchen door creaked open behind her. Christopher stood framed in the light from the back of the house. On a tray stood two flowery China cups and saucers, an ornate teapot and strainer on a stand with, incongruously, a carton of milk. He saw her looking at the tray. 'I know, I'm sorry, but I broke the jug a while back and haven't yet replaced it.' He indicated with his head to the sitting room. 'Please. Do go in and sit.'

But Janice wasn't looking at the tea things or milk carton. It was the front door keys and her mobile phone that were also on the tray, which caught her eye. He'd lifted her phone from her bag.

Janice sank into a brown velour-covered winged armchair, defeated. Her brain focused on the windows to the front, but some sort of shrub blocked a view of the street. It was hopeless.

Meanwhile, Christopher fussed with the tea things.

She let her eyes go round the room, taking in the books and the few ornaments, the sort of thing you might get as a job lot in Ikea or the Next homeware department. She needed to distract him. Keep him talking. 'Your neighbour said you saw your mum regularly. I didn't realise.'

'She never said?'

'No.'

'That would have been Roger's doing.'

'Roger?'

He smiled. 'He saw himself as guardian of the family morals.'

'Sorry?'

'Sugar?'

'What? No, thank you. Roger didn't say anything about you.'

'He was the one who tracked me down. Told Mum, even though he'd been instrumental in keeping us apart.'

'Can you explain?'

'What do you know about me?'

'Not a lot.' She sipped the tea. There had to be a way to raise the alarm. Maybe if she really screamed, or threw a book or ornament through the window. 'You had a twin, Colin. You were older than Roger. You left home and never came back. When I first went out with Roger, it was said you'd disappeared. When his... your father died,' our father, she thought, feeling sick, 'Roger said he was going to try and find you both, but his mother stopped him. When she died, he said he'd try again; he talked about using an agency, but I didn't know he'd done anything. That's pretty much it.'

He sat back in his chair, a mirror of hers. 'No one explained why I left? What happened? Why I kept away?'

She shook her head.

He sighed. 'It was like this…' He stopped. The doorbell rang once, twice, then there was a banging on the door. 'I'd better get this. Please pour yourself a refill.'

Her heart rose. He left the phone on the tray as he moved into the hall. As soon as he was out of sight, she took two strides to pick up the phone and fumbled with the code to unlock it. She had just found and pressed Thorne's number when Christopher reappeared. Behind him stood Inspector Thorne, holding up his phone with her number identified as the caller.

Christopher smiled. 'Oh, you found your phone. Good. It had fallen on the floor.' He ushered in the policeman and constable. 'Quite a party. Shall I make some tea, Sergeant?'

As Christopher disappeared, Thorne tilted his head and held Janice's gaze. 'You know your half-brother, then? Why didn't you say?'

'I've only just met him. He…'

Thorne held up a hand. 'Shall we wait until Mr Scrutt comes back? Just so we can hear everyone's side of the story?'

Janice sank back, shutting her eyes. The relief of seeing the policeman made the idea of explaining why she was there all the harder.

After what seemed to Janice like an hour, but was less than five minutes, Christopher had provided everyone with tea, opened a tin of biscuits and dragged in two kitchen chairs for the policemen to sit on. 'Well, how may I help?'

Thorne looked at Janice. 'We managed to access your husband's laptop. It hadn't been wiped. From that we found the investigation agency and details of Mr Scrutt here. What about you? Did you know which agency to go to?'

She shook her head once, incapable of speech. She was conscious of Christopher smiling in the way she was beginning to think was his default expression. Maybe he wasn't so much creepy as simple. 'I found the man who sold the second typewriter. He gave me this address.'

Thorne's eyebrow rose a fraction, before he sighed deeply. 'Mr Scrutt, I -'

'I call myself Parsons, Inspector. My mother's maiden name. To begin with it was through an understandable reluctance to be found and then, well, it became more difficult to explain. I've meant to have it made official, but I've not bothered. I don't drive and have no passport.' He shrugged. 'Mostly it's fine, though with these modern checks, it is becoming more inconvenient.' The smile seemed to droop a little. 'So, if you would, I'd prefer Parsons though, of course, feel free to call me Christopher.' He positively beamed at that.

Thorne nodded. 'Let me fill in some background so all of us,' he looked at Janice, 'are on the same page. Mrs Scrutt's husband, Roger, died of an apparent heart attack.'

'I heard. He came to visit. After he tracked me down. I don't suppose it was that hard, what with me living in the same town I was born in and still having to use Scrutt from time to time.'

'Did he say why?'

'My father had died. I didn't know, but then we never got on.' He shook his head, a rather sad gesture, Janice thought. 'My mother hadn't dared try and find me when he was alive. His temper was…' it looked like he was struggling for the right word, 'incendiary.' He nodded as if he approved of his own choice. 'As I understood it, my mother wanted to restore relations, though Roger wasn't keen. He told me he didn't want her upset any more than she had been. He always did treat her like a child. But she insisted and he fixed for us to meet. After that we met occasionally. He came the first couple of times and every now and then afterwards.' He glanced at Janice, nodding again.

Thorne caught the gesture. 'Janice?'

'I knew nothing. She said she went to see a friend. I had no idea what Roger, what either of them was doing.'

Christopher smiled broadly. 'As I was saying just before you got here, Inspector, he wanted to keep my existence secret, especially it seems from his wife. He told me to stay away or he wouldn't allow mother and me to meet again.'

Thorne looked up from making a note. 'Did he say why? Did you know?'

'Oh, I'm the black sheep, Inspector. I think I'm probably contagious.' There was that smile again.

Thorne and Janice waited, but Christopher didn't elaborate. Thorne looked out of the window and then back to Christopher. 'Roger's death wouldn't have involved us, normally, but after your mother died, the house, her house, was sold. By Mrs Scrutt here. The new owners carried out some work that involved digging in the garden. They discovered a pit and in it were the carcasses of two pigs and the bones of a human hand. We think it was your brother Colin's and he must have been fed to them.'

Thorne paused, astonished at Christopher's reaction. He was laughing, almost hysterical.

The inspector looked at Janice who shrugged, equally bemused. It took Christopher several moments to regain some composure. As he did so, he slowly and laboriously rolled up his sleeve.

'I have a prosthetic, Inspector. I'm lucky to live near a hospital with a state-of-the-art facility for modern prosthetics and robotics. If you are familiar with them, you'll spot it immediately, but neither you nor Janice have, I suspect, come across these wonders.' He reached out and carefully but successfully picked up the mug of tea and moved it to his lips. 'I tend to use my good hand, but really I can do nearly all everyday tasks that don't involve too much strength work with this.' He wiped his eyes again. 'Colin and I were identical twins, so we have the same DNA. It could be his, but since my arm was cut off by my father and fed to the pigs, I guess it's most likely to be mine.'

Janice covered her mouth with her hand. 'He cut off your arm? Why?'

Christopher looked at her. 'Family shame is a strong emotion.' He paused, apparently letting that sink in, before continuing. 'I've thought about it a lot. I don't think he meant to hurt me quite so badly, but when he confronted me and I confirmed the truth, the chainsaw was the nearest tool and he had completely lost it. It was dressed up as an accident and I knew it would kill Mother if she knew the truth, so I went along with it. The hospital wanted to know if the arm had been saved, but we both said it had gone in with the pigs and been eaten. It looks like the old man must have kept it. Sick sod.'

Thorne rubbed his face and looked at the constable next to him. 'We will need to verify this. Do you remember the hospital?'

Christopher gave him the details and the date. 'You said it was in a pit in the garden? I wonder why he buried it there.'

'The pit also contained some other items that were put in later.'

'Really? Such as?'

Thorne hesitated, then said, 'An old Corona typewriter and a letter addressed to Mrs Scrutt here. We have no explanation why.'

'No, well, that would be curious, wouldn't it? I mean...'

Janice couldn't stop herself. 'You bought one. A typewriter. From the shop in town.' She looked at the inspector. 'That's how I found Christopher. Through the shop.'

Christopher looked like he was trying to recall something. 'I did buy a typewriter. An old Corona. Was it a match for the one my father had? There may be something a psychologist would make of my choice. I had this idea of writing down a family history, so at least it wouldn't be completely forgotten.'

'You made me sit at it and get my prints on it!'

Christopher blinked and then frowned briefly. He turned to the inspector. 'Maybe I should explain why my father went for me? I'm sure you want to know.'

'Please.'

'My brother left home six months before me. We were not just brothers, but lovers, Inspector. As you might imagine my father wasn't pleased. Colin knew it was wrong and thought the only way to stop it and deal with the guilt was to leave. I didn't see it like that.

I understand society doesn't approve but…' He trailed off, then rallied. 'I think Father wanted to put all the blame on me. He was furious, throwing accusations around: I forced Colin; I was the cause of his distress and why he left; I wanted to shame the family. After the attack I understood I couldn't stay, and I think it suited him and therefore the rest of the family to say we had fallen out for unspecified reasons and just left. I was pleased, after I'd gone, that I got out when I did. If I had stayed, I think he might have killed me or me him.'

'And Roger knew about this?'

'At the time, no. He was still a youngster - fourteen, maybe - but I expect Father told him some version of the truth. When he found me again, he wouldn't say what he'd been told the fact I was gay that was the problem.'

Thorne nodded. 'And Colin? What happened to him?'

Christopher looked at the back of his good hand. 'Even though we were twins, he was so much more impressionable. When he saw what had happened to me, he blamed himself. It destroyed us. Him.'

There was a silence before Thorne prompted him.

'No, I don't know where he went, Inspector. I think he may have committed suicide. It's not so hard around here, just to walk into the sea.' He shook his head. 'I tried to find out where he might have gone. My attempts went cold in Whitstable. He was in a tatty B&B for a time. I can give you the details to follow up on.'

Thorne nodded. 'And you know nothing of the pit and the arm and Roger's death?'

'No, Inspector, why would I? Once Father was dead, I was happy to see Mother – she was old and frail and not in a good place mentally – but I've long since moved on.'

'And the typewriter? Do you still have it?'

'I gave it to Roger.'

'You what?' Janice exploded. 'You can't have done.'

Christopher shook his head. 'Why not? I had it out when he brought Mother and when she saw it, she was delighted. She asked if it was Father's - his had gone missing long since, she said – and when I told her I'd found it in this shop, she asked if I could try and get her a copy, too, so she could type her letters on it. She was an inveterate correspondent. I told her to take the one I'd bought and she was delighted. Roger said he'd get it serviced – the letter "p" was rather inclined to stick. That was the last I saw of it.'

Thorne looked at Janice, waiting for her to speak.

'I've never seen it, Inspector. As I said there was one like it in the attic at my mother-in-law's house.' She felt ill.

Thorne sighed, 'I think we might leave it there. Mrs Scrutt, could we have a few words, please? Mr Parsons, thank you for your help. We may need to talk again.'

'Of course.' He showed them out.

Standing on the street, Thorne looked livid. 'What are you doing here? What's going on?'

Janice felt exhausted. 'I thought I could maybe find out who had made me sit at that typewriter and get my prints on it, at the fair Roger brought me to. If I got a name or something, I was going to tell you, but the hotel where it was held sent me to the shop and they remembered him buying an old Corona, so I came to see his house and -'

'Why?'

She fought back tears. 'I don't know. I just wanted to see him, to check if he really was Christopher. He was using that other name, so I couldn't be sure.' She wiped her face. 'He was away, but his neighbour said they were close and she had a key and needed someone to feed his cat as she was off, too.'

Thorne held up a hand. 'Are you listening to yourself? Do you really expect me…?'

'Speak to her! To Godfrey, the man who lives there,' she waved at the house on the other side. 'He'll confirm I was to feed the cat.'

'I'm not interested in how you got inside his house, but why? Why not call me? You must realise what this looks like.'

'What do you mean?'

'So far, Mr Scrutt or Parsons is telling a plausible if awful story of abuse, of being driven away. He may have known about your father's affair, too, your birth and not want to say. Your husband seems to have helped perpetuate that situation. Whereas your version always seems to be far-fetched. I'm wondering if you aren't trying to frame him in some way, maybe for the death of your husband. What did he tell you about Christopher and Colin? Did he pass on his hatred of his brother?'

'Roger didn't do hate. That wasn't the sort of person he was.'

Thorne blew out a large breath. 'We need to continue this at the station with your solicitor present.'

'Are you going to search his house? He has a shed that's full of-'

'Stop. You were in his shed? Without his permission?'

'Yes, I just thought...'

'What? That if you go somewhere where there might be clues to something illegal, then your presence will only enhance the forensic evidence? You've contaminated the scene. Did you go into every room?'

She nodded dumbly.

'Whatever we might find, there will always be the argument that you put it there.' He turned away and then back. 'The autopsy on your husband will be done in two days. I suggest you go home and stay away from here and wait until I call you.'

*

Janice sat at her kitchen table. She felt like a zombie having had little to no sleep, wondering what Thorne was going to do with her. Eventually, a call came asking her to come to the station. Her solicitor accompanied her and was equally if not quite so volubly sceptical of Janice's explanation. Thorne was accompanied by a uniformed female officer called Cilla, who hardly looked up and took copious notes even though the recording machinery ran throughout. She tried once again to explain everything that had happened since she had visited the hotel in Margate, but it sounded more and more unlikely, even to her ears.

Thorne sat back in his chair, barely moving throughout her monologue. When she finished, he leant forward. 'Christopher told the truth about his arm. In so far as the current treatment is concerned, but the hospital that originally treated him has shut and the records from that time aren't available. His specialist confirms the approximate age of the injury however, so we have no reason to disbelieve the timing.' He looked up as a uniformed constable knocked and came in with coffee. 'It also appears true that he uses Parsons, but he hasn't applied for any sort of official change and all his official records are in the name of Scrutt. He has lived at that address for fifteen years and the neighbours confirm he's a quiet neighbour if a little obsessive.'

'The neighbour, the woman, had some sort of relationship with him.'

'Indeed, so they both said, but it's not recent, maybe two years ago. He's not been known to have any sort of,' Thorne coughed, 'companion. The male neighbour says he was regularly visited by an elderly woman, but he didn't know who. She was sometimes dropped off and picked up by a man fitting Roger's description. So far as we can tell, his story fits.'

'What about the man in the typewriter shop?'

'He says he remembers the machine more than the man who bought it. He wasn't especially helpful.' Thorne paused. When Janice said no more, he shifted a file from the bottom of the heap he had brought with him. 'Roger's body, as you know, was exhumed last week. The toxicology tests have been done.' He looked over Janice's shoulder. 'There are traces of adrenaline in quantities that suggest he was injected. This, coupled with the known medical issues he had, suggest he was deliberately killed.'

Janice felt a tear slip down her cheek. Killed? Surely not? He couldn't have been.

The policeman looked at her. 'I mentioned we had his laptop. Did you use it?'

She nodded. Of course, she did. It was the family machine.

'It appears that someone used it to determine the best way to obtain and administer adrenaline. Can you explain that?'

'No. No, I can't.'

Thorne nodded. 'Obviously this is currently circumstantial, but can you see the way it's pointing?'

'You think I killed him? Why?'

Thorne shrugged. 'There might be any number of reasons.'

Janice let her head droop. Her solicitor briefly put a hand on her shoulder. She said, 'What are you intending to do with my client?'

'For now, nothing. We will continue to garner evidence. We would like her to voluntarily surrender her passport and agree to stay in the neighbourhood, but she is free to go.'

Janice nodded, not that she understood anything. What was happening to her?

*

Christopher looked through his small bag. Water, the cup that Janice had used, the transfer paper: check. As he turned out of the cul-de-sac where he lived, he pulled up the hood on his anorak. Fifty yards ahead, he turned into the narrow path between numbers 55 and 57 and headed quickly away from the road. When he was sure no one was able to see him from either direction, he bent and lifted the fence panel. To anyone passing it looked like a normal panel, but this one hinged inward. Quickly, he stepped off the path and onto the grass. The panel swung back and clicked in place. Without wasting time but, in the knowledge no one could overlook him, he crossed the overgrown garden of Mrs Tomlins, a woman he had befriended and whose garden had proved a perfect access to the allotment.

It was more awkward, scaling the allotment fence at the back of her garden, but the old hawthorns provided enough of a barrier. Once through those the backdoor of his shed could be reached in a step. No one had yet seen him. If they did, all he would do was shake his fly and look sheepish. The male need to pee was an easy excuse to be skulking in some bushes.

'Okay?' The other man looked up as Christopher entered.

'Sweet as the proverbial. Here you go.' He held out the bag. 'One perfect set of prints.'

'She didn't notice the oil on the cup?'

'Scared shitless. All she could do was keep looking at her phone.' Christopher laughed. 'Can you sort it?'

The other man looked up and nodded. 'Sure. Where will you leave the syringe?'

'In my shed. With the bottle of dye. Where it's been all along. I'll tell the nice policeman I found it. It'll be such an obvious plant, but I don't think she's the sharpest knife in the drawer, so the police won't be surprised.' Christopher looked at the table where a small book – "The Law and Practice of Wills and Estates" - sat. 'How soon before we can challenge the will?'

'Soon as she's charged. They'll not let her inherit our money from Roger if she killed him. It'll come to you,' the man smiled, 'us.'

Christopher returned the smile and bent to kiss his brother.

Printed in Great Britain
by Amazon

23458671R00126